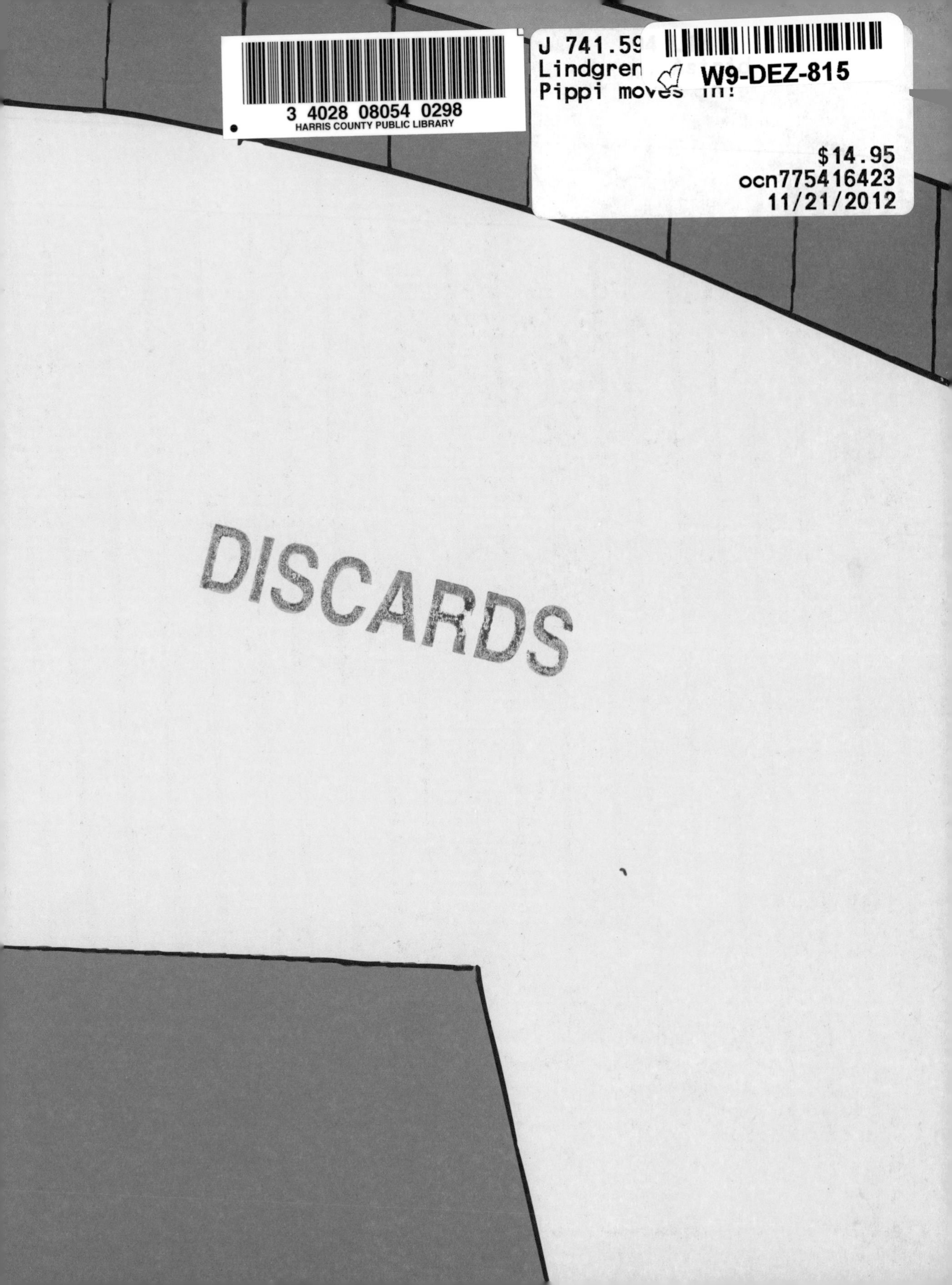

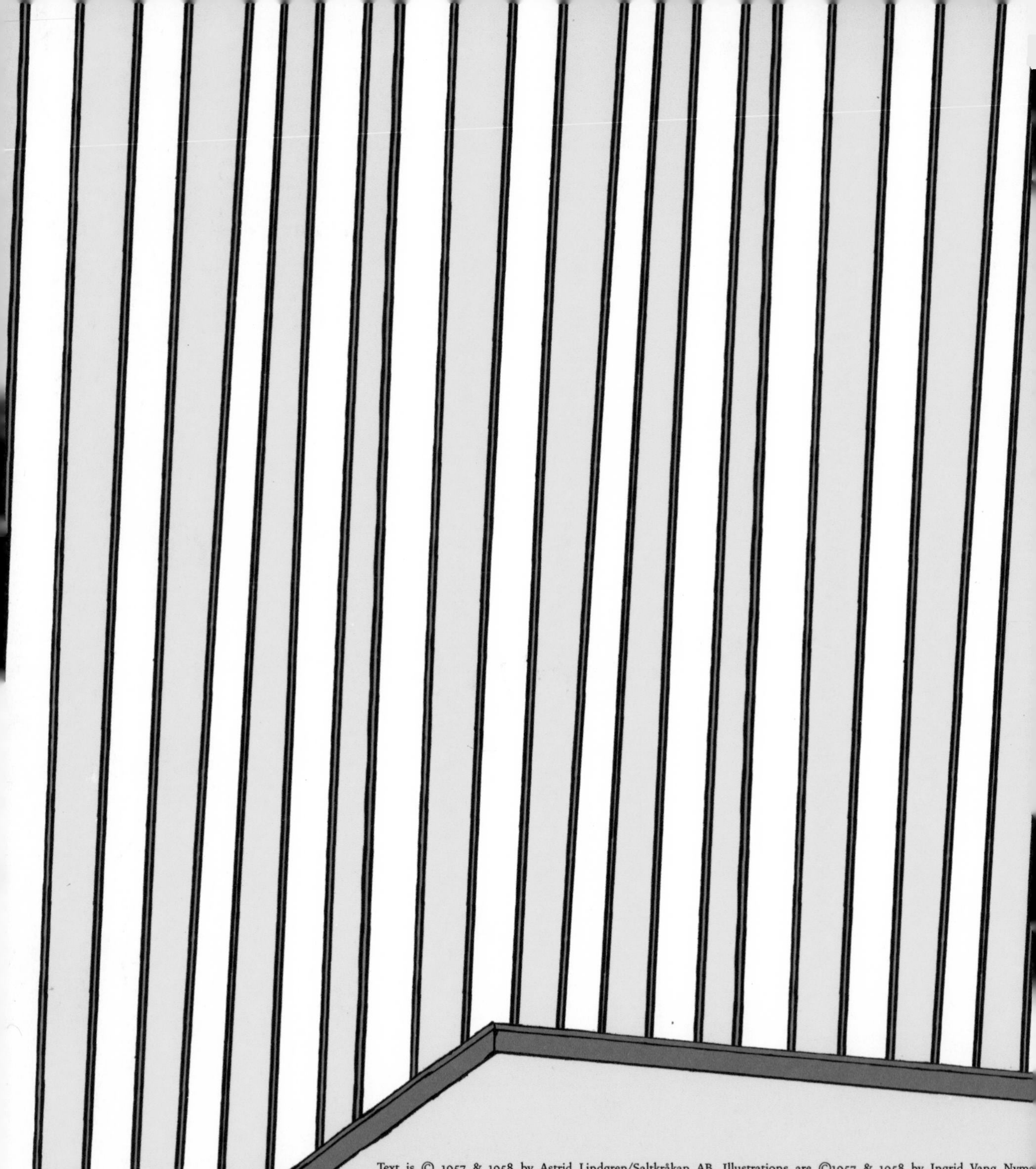

Enfant is
imprint of Drawn & Quarterly. Originally published as *Pippi Flytarr in Och Andra Serier* in 2010 by Rabén & Sjögren (ISBN 978-91-29-67529-
The translation of this book was funded by the Swedish Arts Council. Drawn & Quarterly; Post Office Box 48056; Montreal, QC; Canada; H
4S8; www.drawnandquarterly.com First hardcover edition: September 2012. Printed in Singapore. 10 9 8 7 6 5 4 3 2 1. Library and Archives Cana
Cataloguing in Publication. Lindgren, Astrid, 1907-2002. *Pippi Moves In* / Astrid Lindgren and Ingrid Vang Nyman. ISBN 978-1-77046-09
1. Graphic novels. I. Vang-Nyman, Ingrid, 1916-1959 II. Title. PZ7.7.L55P56 2012 j741.5'9485 C2012-902520-8. Distributed in the USA by Far
Straus and Giroux; 18 West 18th St; New York, NY 10011; Orders: 888.330.8477; Distributed in Canada by Raincoast Books; 2440 Viking Way; Vancouver,
v6v 1n2; Orders: 800.663.5714. Distributed in the United Kingdom by Publishers Group U.K.; 63-66 Hatton Garden London; EC1N 8LE; info@pguk.co

Pippi

Moves in!

**by Astrid Lindgren &
Ingrid Vang Nyman**

Translated by Tiina Nunnally

ENFANT

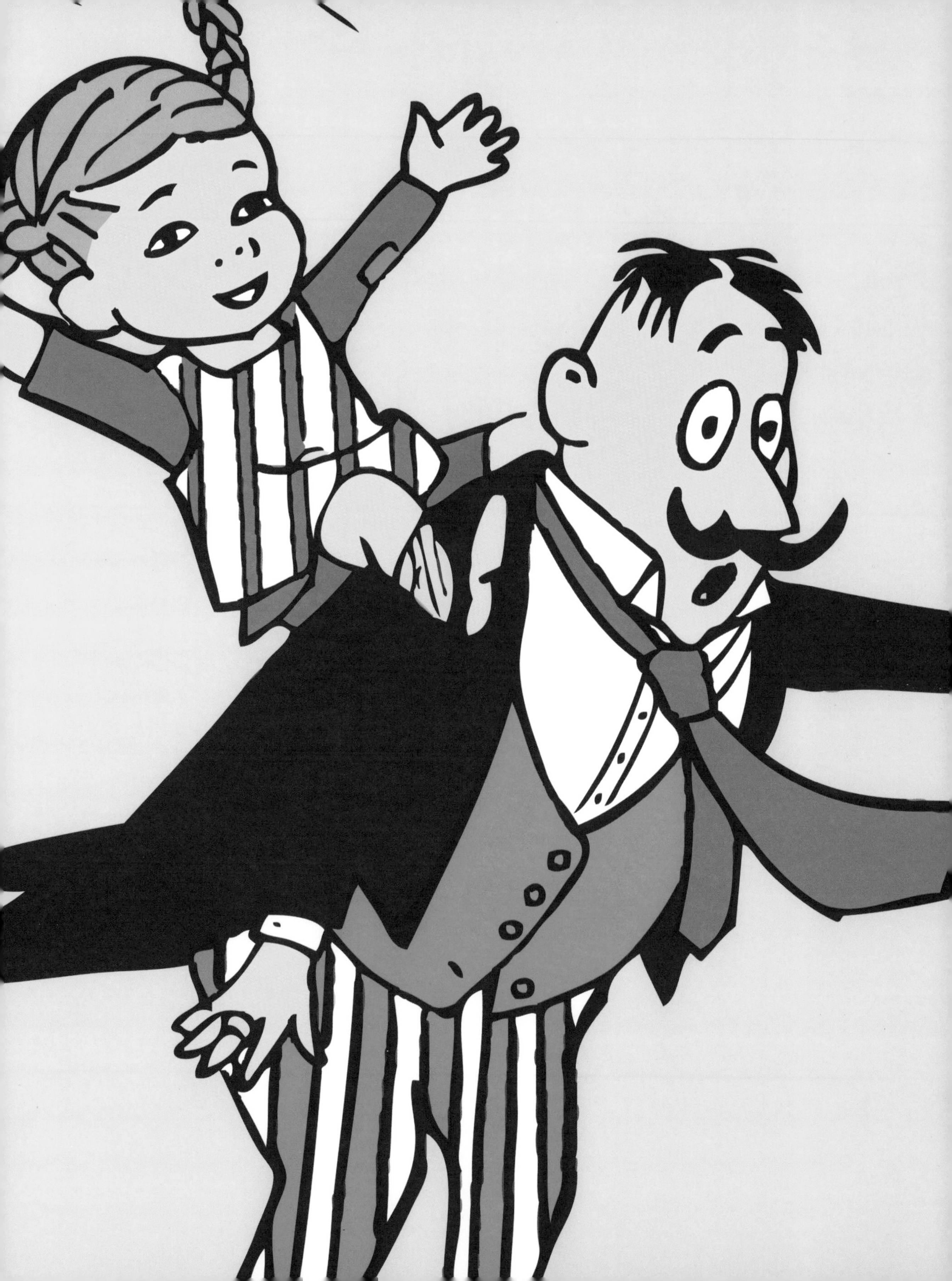

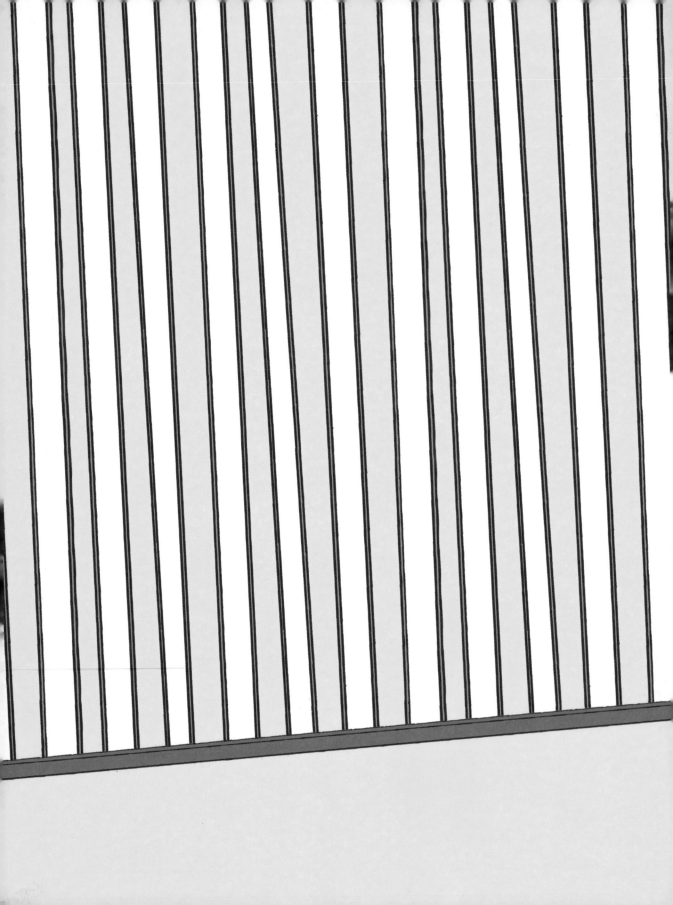

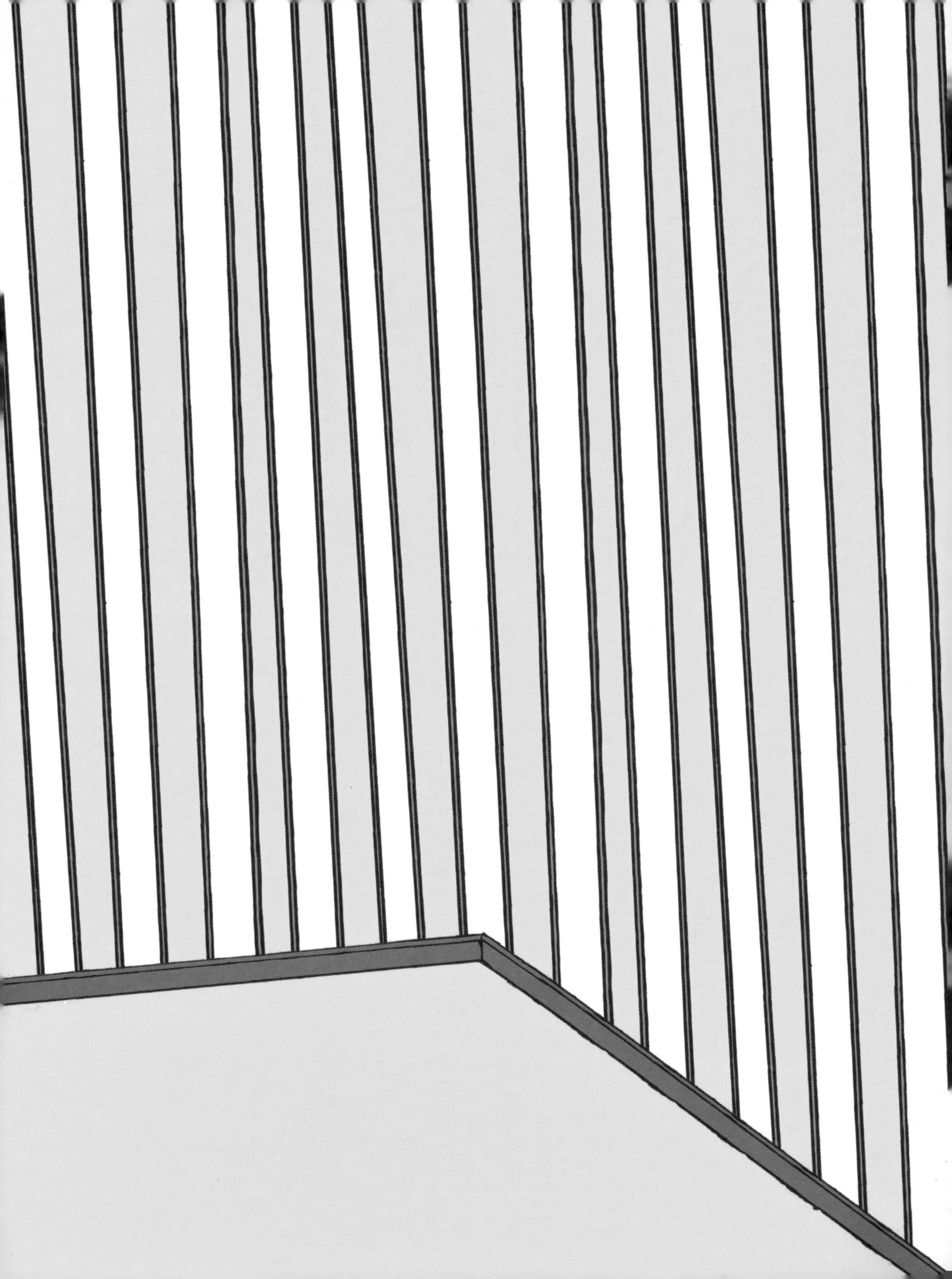

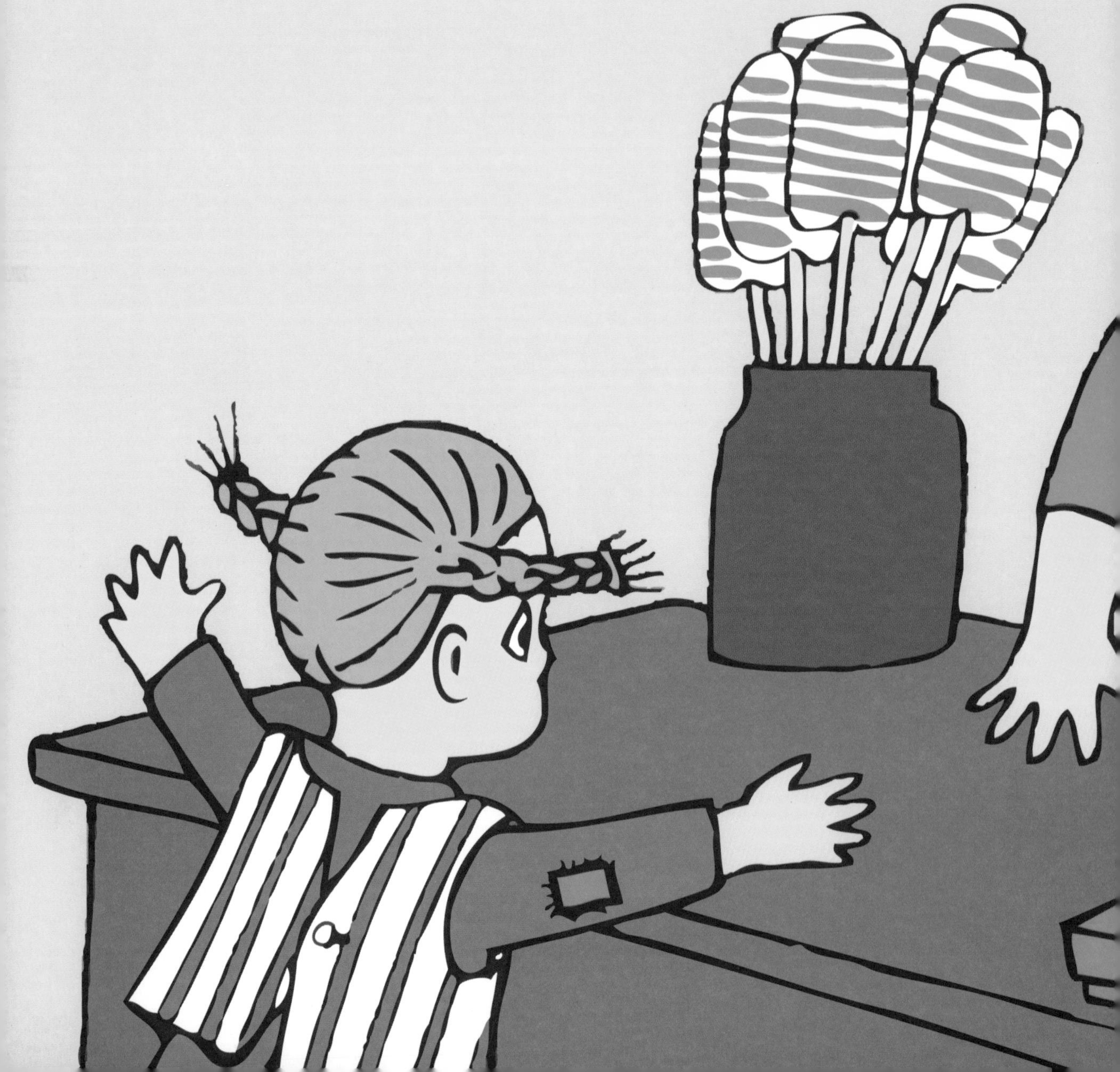

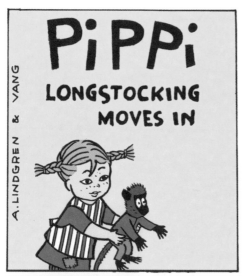

PiPPi
LONGSTOCKING MOVES IN

A. LINDGREN & VANG

WHAT SHOULD WE DO, TOMMY?

I DON'T KNOW. THERE'S NOTHING FUN TO DO.

THIS IS THE PRETTY HOUSE WHERE TOMMY AND ANNIKA LIVE.

NEXT DOOR TO TOMMY AND ANNIKA THERE'S AN EMPTY HOUSE. NOBODY LIVES THERE.

IT'S SO STUPID THAT NOBODY LIVES THERE.

YEAH, SOMEONE SHOULD MOVE IN. SOMEONE WITH KIDS.

CAN YOU BELIEVE IT, ANNIKA? SHE'S LIFTING A HORSE!

NOBODY CAN LIFT A HORSE!

I CAN.

ONE NIGHT, A LITTLE GIRL MOVES INTO THE EMPTY HOUSE. TOMMY AND ANNIKA DON'T KNOW IT YET, BUT SHE'S THE STRONGEST IN THE WORLD.

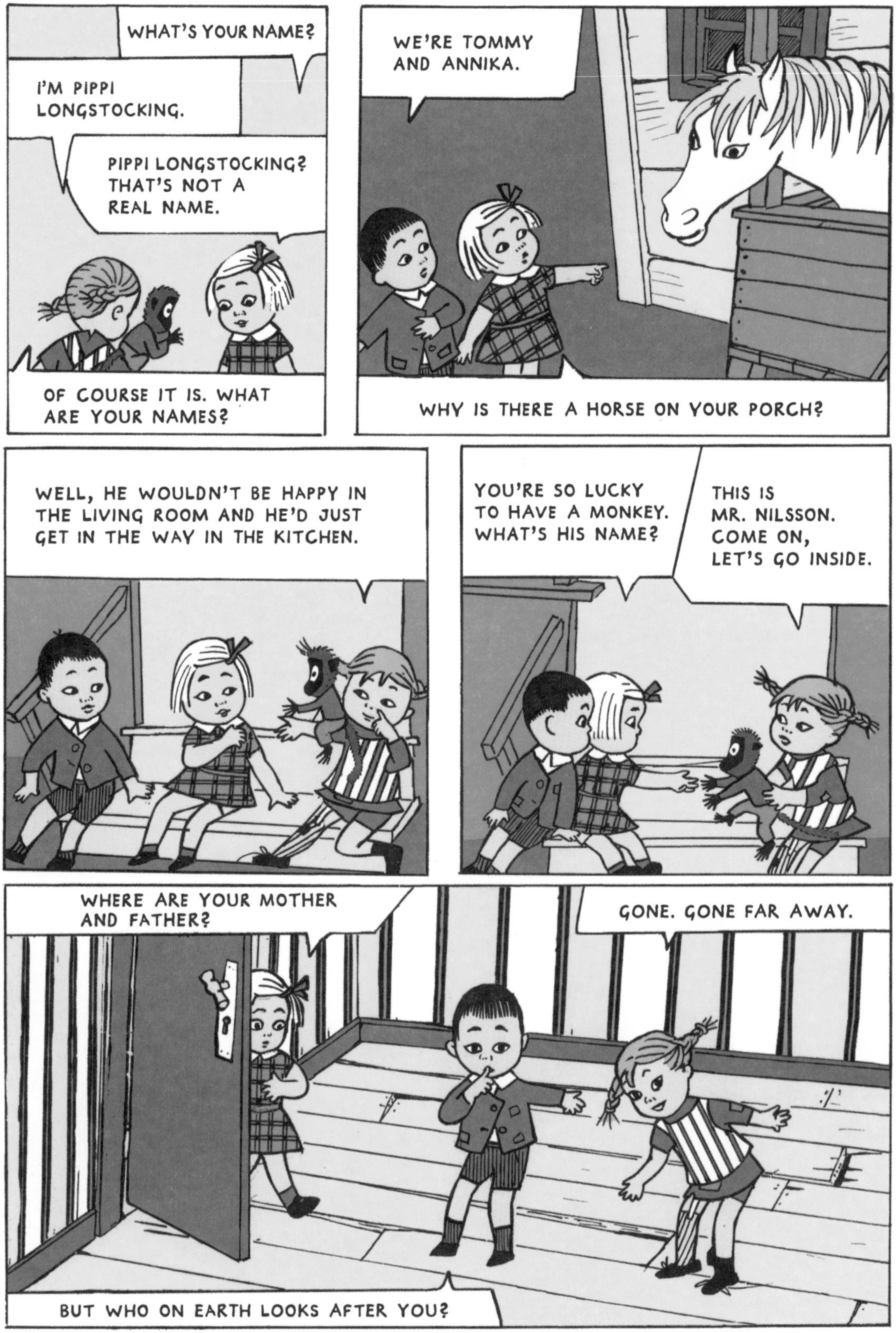
WHAT'S YOUR NAME?
I'M PIPPI LONGSTOCKING.
PIPPI LONGSTOCKING? THAT'S NOT A REAL NAME.
OF COURSE IT IS. WHAT ARE YOUR NAMES?
WE'RE TOMMY AND ANNIKA.
WHY IS THERE A HORSE ON YOUR PORCH?
WELL, HE WOULDN'T BE HAPPY IN THE LIVING ROOM AND HE'D JUST GET IN THE WAY IN THE KITCHEN.
YOU'RE SO LUCKY TO HAVE A MONKEY. WHAT'S HIS NAME?
THIS IS MR. NILSSON. COME ON, LET'S GO INSIDE.
WHERE ARE YOUR MOTHER AND FATHER?
GONE. GONE FAR AWAY.
BUT WHO ON EARTH LOOKS AFTER YOU?

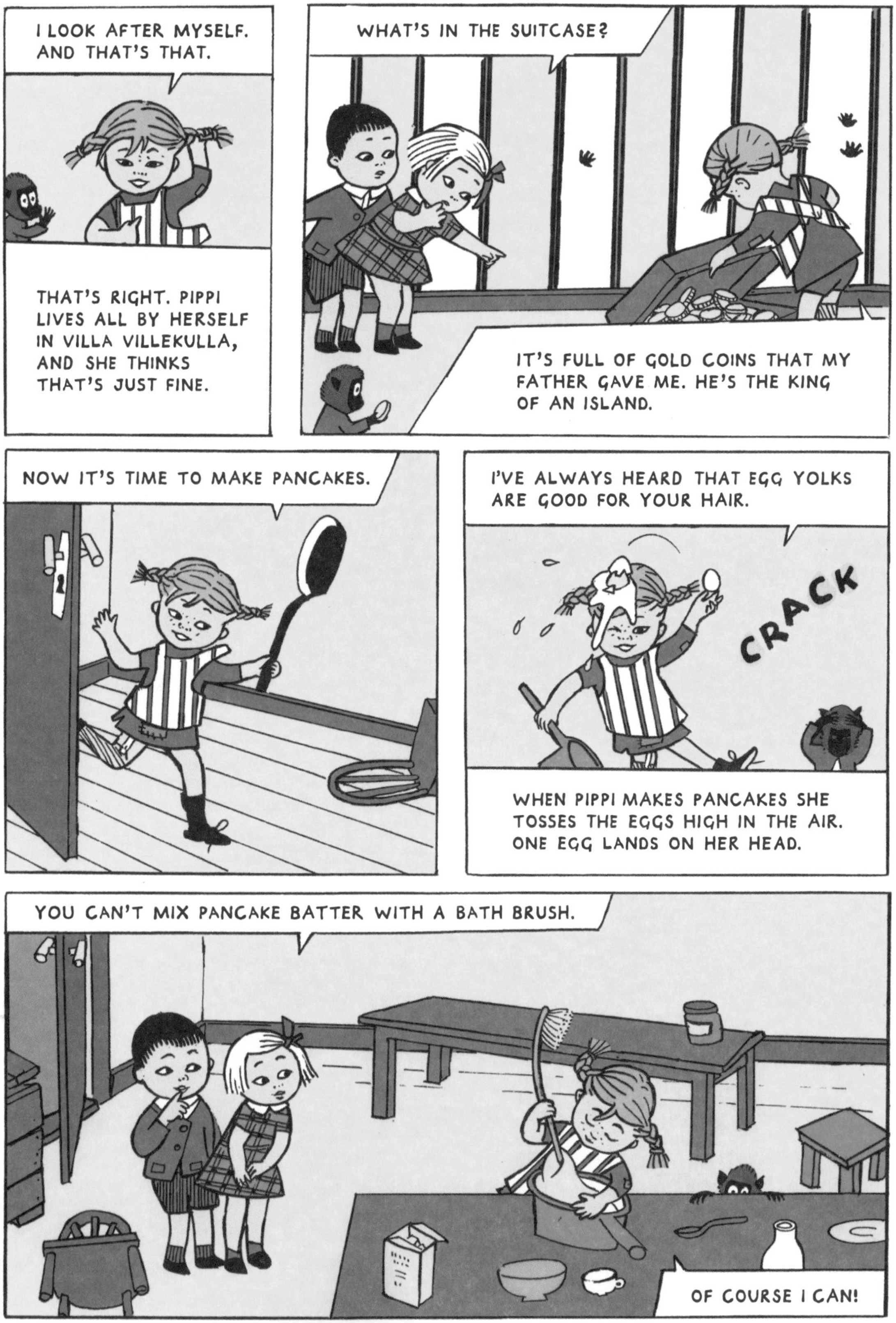
I LOOK AFTER MYSELF. AND THAT'S THAT.
THAT'S RIGHT. PIPPI LIVES ALL BY HERSELF IN VILLA VILLEKULLA, AND SHE THINKS THAT'S JUST FINE.
WHAT'S IN THE SUITCASE?
IT'S FULL OF GOLD COINS THAT MY FATHER GAVE ME. HE'S THE KING OF AN ISLAND.
NOW IT'S TIME TO MAKE PANCAKES.
I'VE ALWAYS HEARD THAT EGG YOLKS ARE GOOD FOR YOUR HAIR.
CRACK
WHEN PIPPI MAKES PANCAKES SHE TOSSES THE EGGS HIGH IN THE AIR. ONE EGG LANDS ON HER HEAD.
YOU CAN'T MIX PANCAKE BATTER WITH A BATH BRUSH.
OF COURSE I CAN!

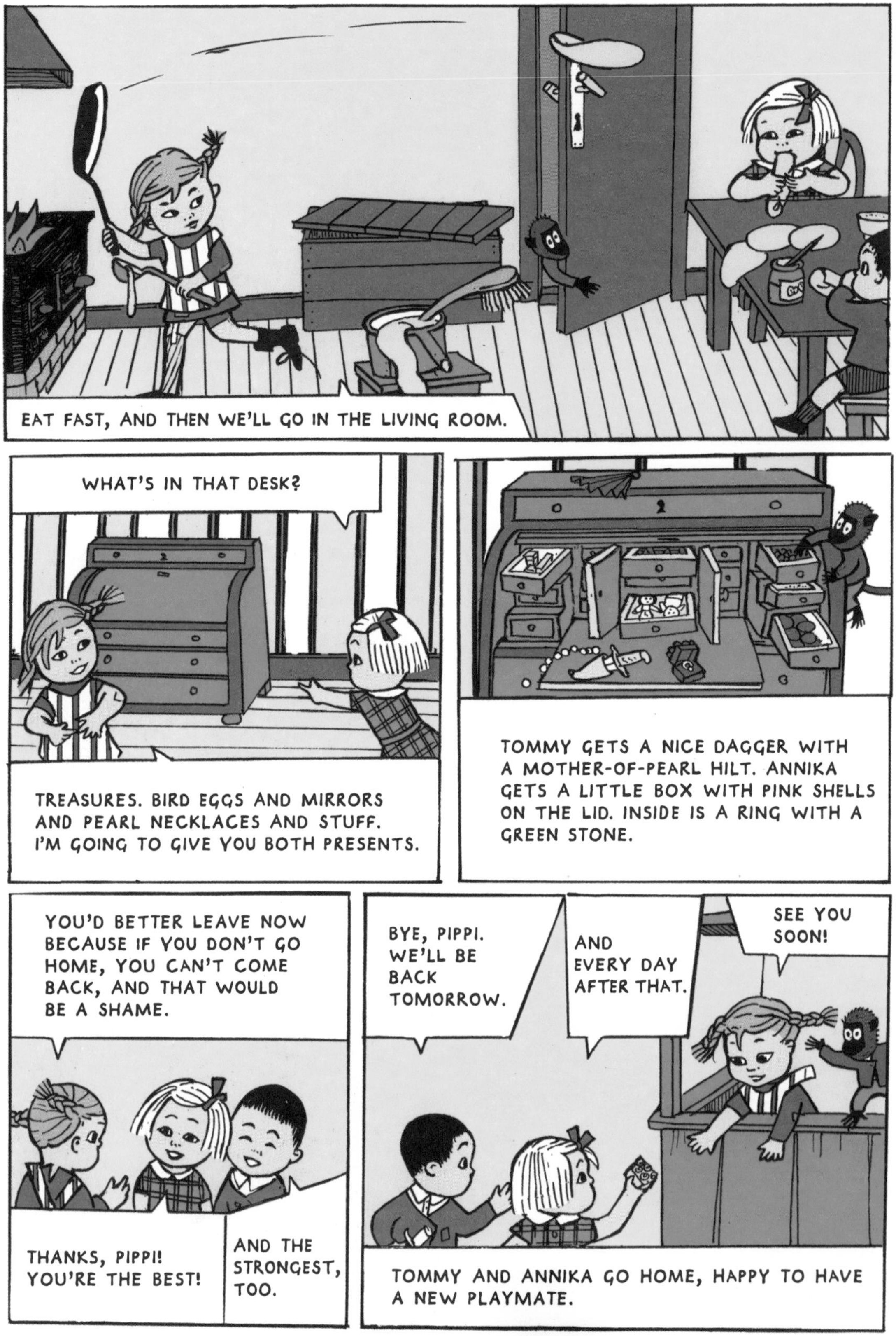
EAT FAST, AND THEN WE'LL GO IN THE LIVING ROOM.
WHAT'S IN THAT DESK?
TREASURES. BIRD EGGS AND MIRRORS AND PEARL NECKLACES AND STUFF. I'M GOING TO GIVE YOU BOTH PRESENTS.
TOMMY GETS A NICE DAGGER WITH A MOTHER-OF-PEARL HILT. ANNIKA GETS A LITTLE BOX WITH PINK SHELLS ON THE LID. INSIDE IS A RING WITH A GREEN STONE.
YOU'D BETTER LEAVE NOW BECAUSE IF YOU DON'T GO HOME, YOU CAN'T COME BACK, AND THAT WOULD BE A SHAME.
THANKS, PIPPI! YOU'RE THE BEST!
AND THE STRONGEST, TOO.
BYE, PIPPI. WE'LL BE BACK TOMORROW.
AND EVERY DAY AFTER THAT.
SEE YOU SOON!
TOMMY AND ANNIKA GO HOME, HAPPY TO HAVE A NEW PLAYMATE.

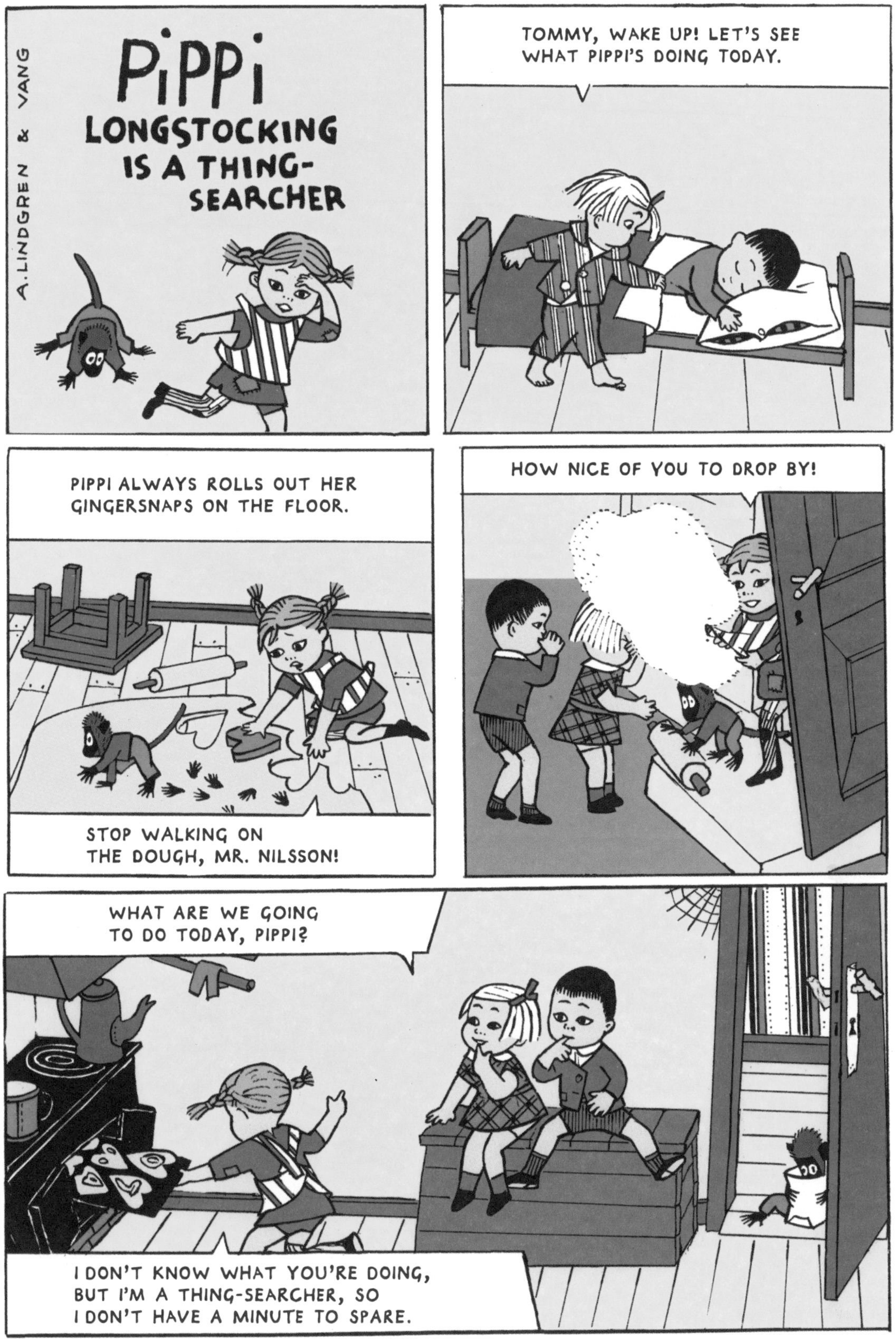
PIPPI LONGSTOCKING IS A THING-SEARCHER
A. LINDGREN & VANG
TOMMY, WAKE UP! LET'S SEE WHAT PIPPI'S DOING TODAY.
PIPPI ALWAYS ROLLS OUT HER GINGERSNAPS ON THE FLOOR.
STOP WALKING ON THE DOUGH, MR. NILSSON!
HOW NICE OF YOU TO DROP BY!
WHAT ARE WE GOING TO DO TODAY, PIPPI?
I DON'T KNOW WHAT YOU'RE DOING, BUT I'M A THING-SEARCHER, SO I DON'T HAVE A MINUTE TO SPARE.

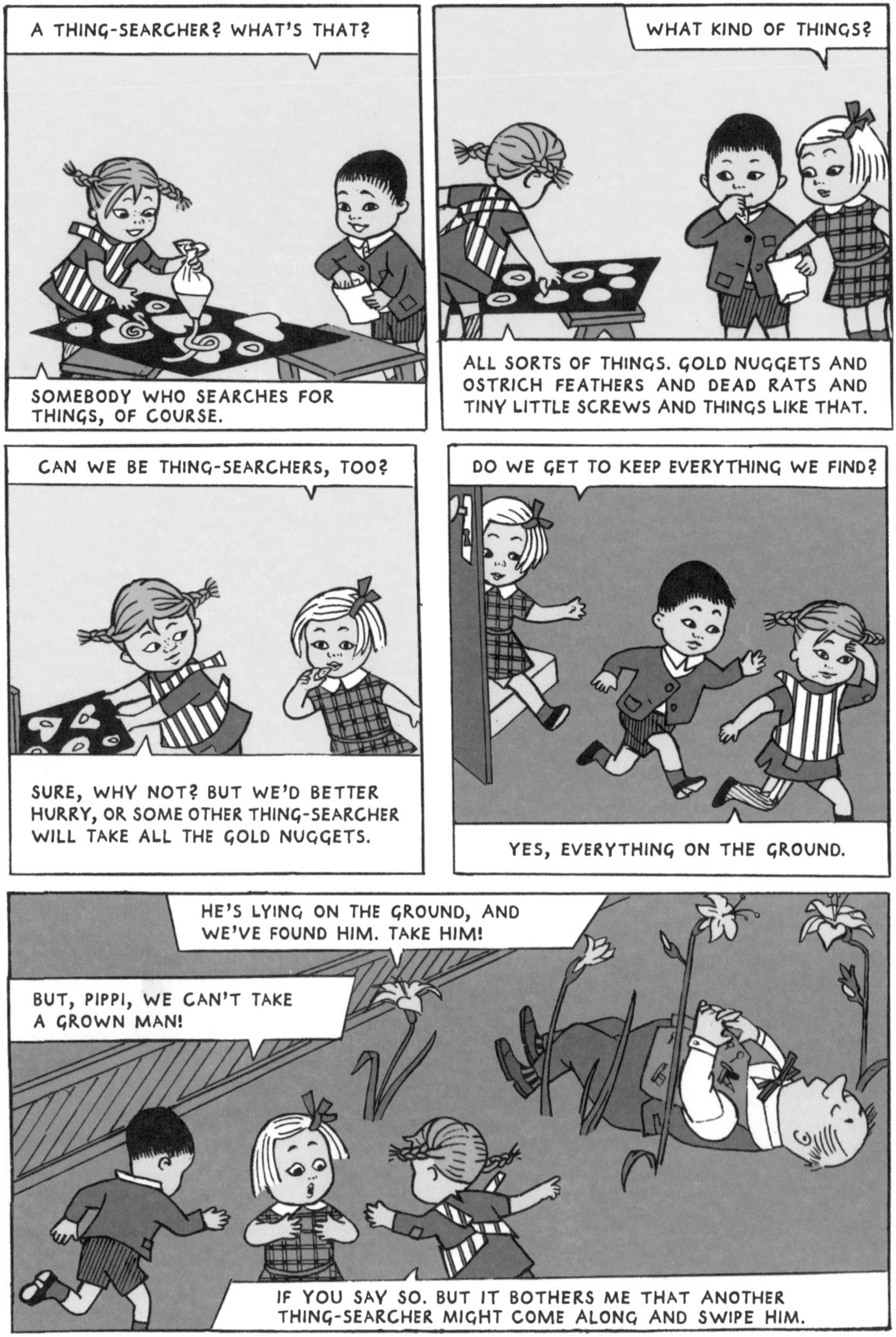
A THING-SEARCHER? WHAT'S THAT?
SOMEBODY WHO SEARCHES FOR THINGS, OF COURSE.
WHAT KIND OF THINGS?
ALL SORTS OF THINGS. GOLD NUGGETS AND OSTRICH FEATHERS AND DEAD RATS AND TINY LITTLE SCREWS AND THINGS LIKE THAT.
CAN WE BE THING-SEARCHERS, TOO?
SURE, WHY NOT? BUT WE'D BETTER HURRY, OR SOME OTHER THING-SEARCHER WILL TAKE ALL THE GOLD NUGGETS.
DO WE GET TO KEEP EVERYTHING WE FIND?
YES, EVERYTHING ON THE GROUND.
HE'S LYING ON THE GROUND, AND WE'VE FOUND HIM. TAKE HIM!
BUT, PIPPI, WE CAN'T TAKE A GROWN MAN!
IF YOU SAY SO. BUT IT BOTHERS ME THAT ANOTHER THING-SEARCHER MIGHT COME ALONG AND SWIPE HIM.

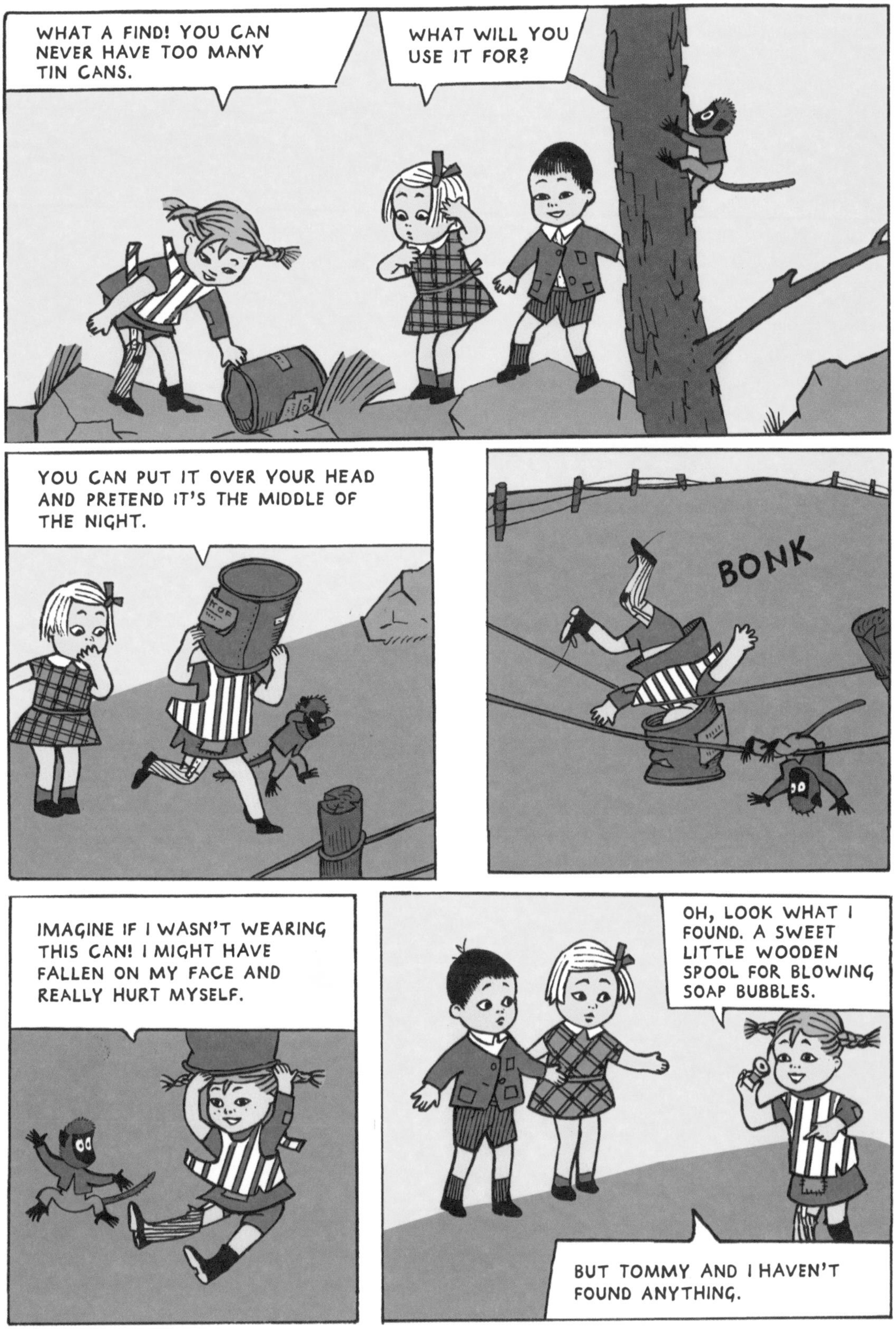
WHAT A FIND! YOU CAN NEVER HAVE TOO MANY TIN CANS.
WHAT WILL YOU USE IT FOR?
YOU CAN PUT IT OVER YOUR HEAD AND PRETEND IT'S THE MIDDLE OF THE NIGHT.
BONK
IMAGINE IF I WASN'T WEARING THIS CAN! I MIGHT HAVE FALLEN ON MY FACE AND REALLY HURT MYSELF.
OH, LOOK WHAT I FOUND. A SWEET LITTLE WOODEN SPOOL FOR BLOWING SOAP BUBBLES.
BUT TOMMY AND I HAVEN'T FOUND ANYTHING.

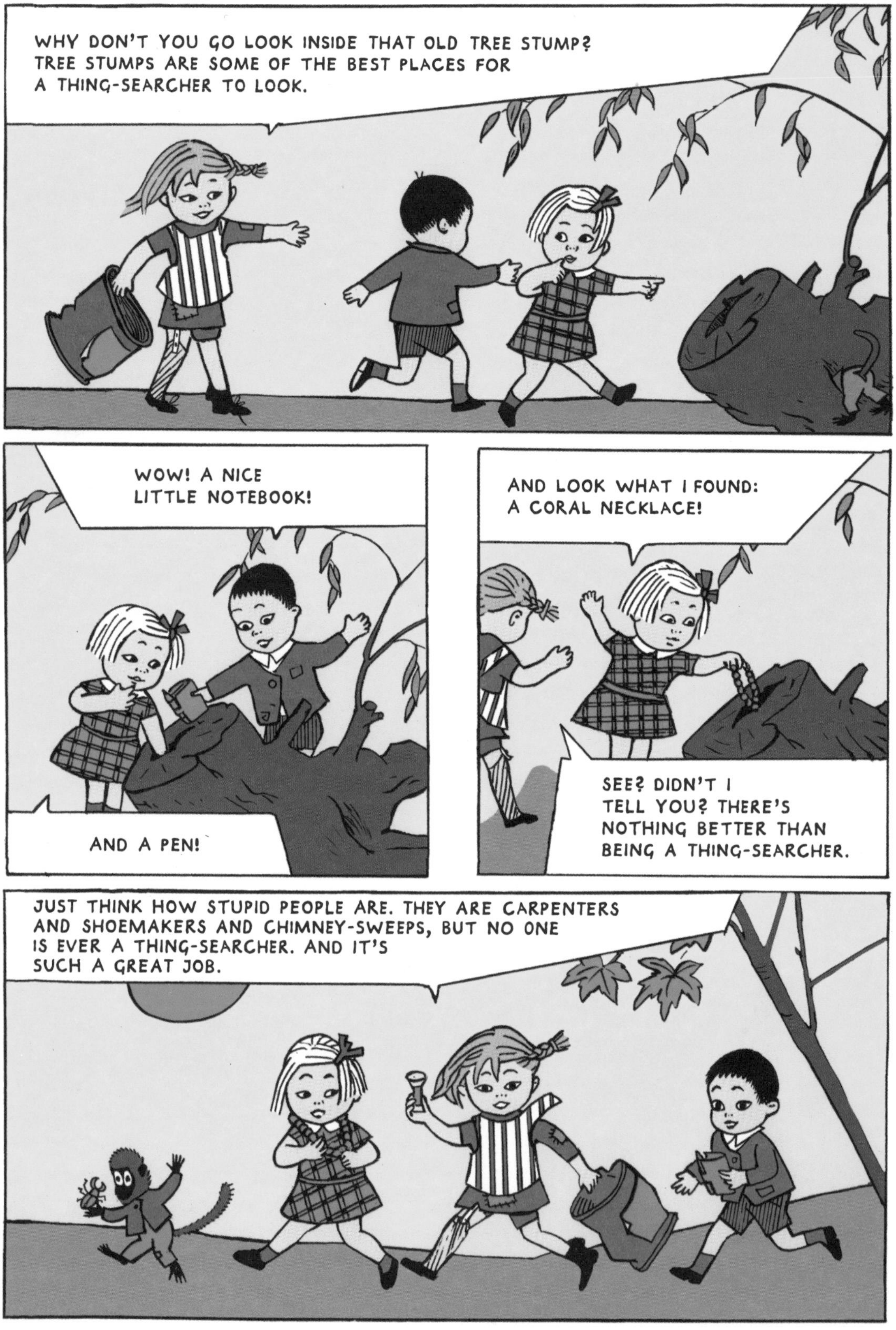
WHY DON'T YOU GO LOOK INSIDE THAT OLD TREE STUMP? TREE STUMPS ARE SOME OF THE BEST PLACES FOR A THING-SEARCHER TO LOOK.
WOW! A NICE LITTLE NOTEBOOK!
AND A PEN!
AND LOOK WHAT I FOUND: A CORAL NECKLACE!
SEE? DIDN'T I TELL YOU? THERE'S NOTHING BETTER THAN BEING A THING-SEARCHER.
JUST THINK HOW STUPID PEOPLE ARE. THEY ARE CARPENTERS AND SHOEMAKERS AND CHIMNEY-SWEEPS, BUT NO ONE IS EVER A THING-SEARCHER. AND IT'S SUCH A GREAT JOB.

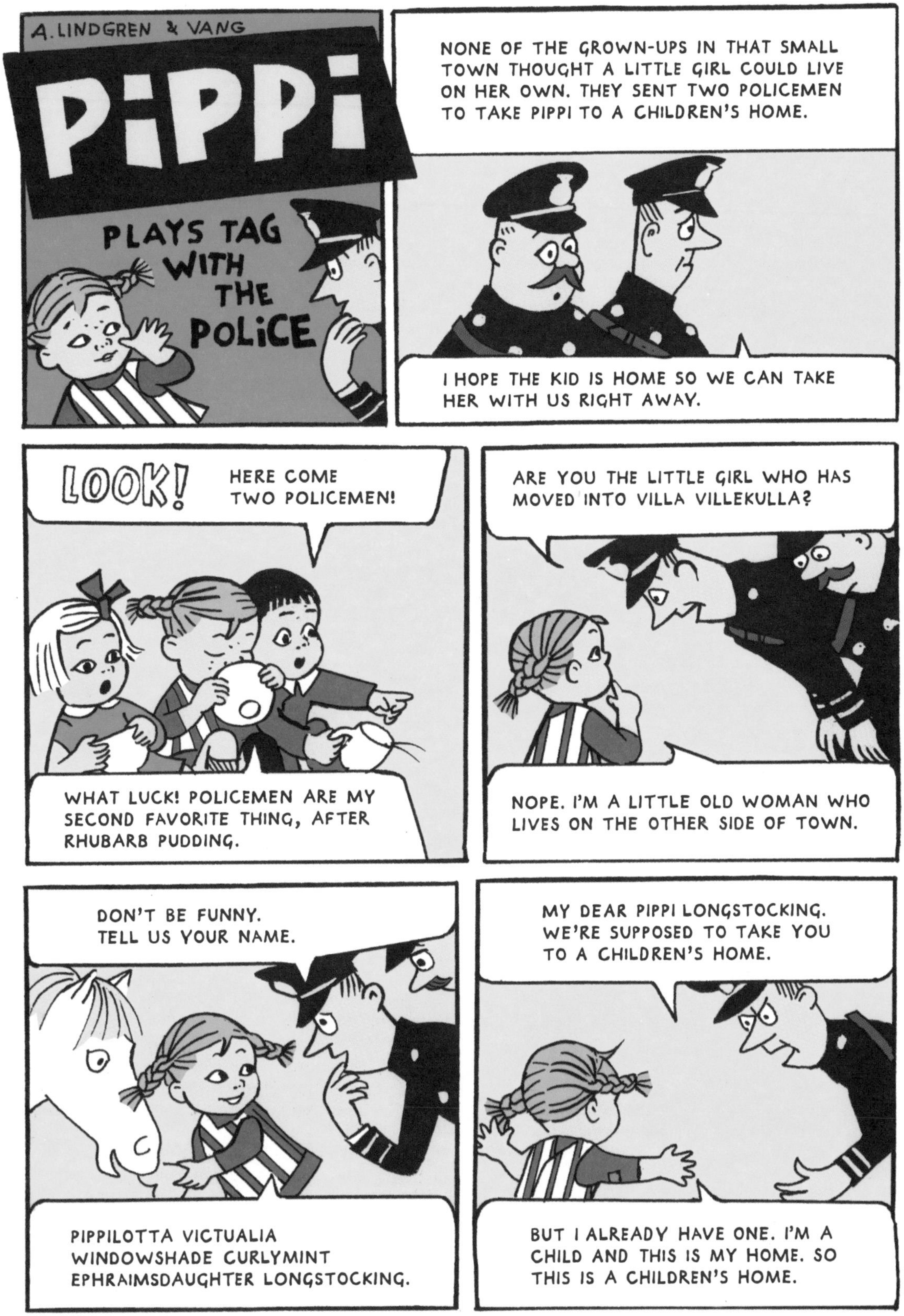

A. LINDGREN & VANG
PiPPi
PLAYS TAG WITH THE POLICE
NONE OF THE GROWN-UPS IN THAT SMALL TOWN THOUGHT A LITTLE GIRL COULD LIVE ON HER OWN. THEY SENT TWO POLICEMEN TO TAKE PIPPI TO A CHILDREN'S HOME.
I HOPE THE KID IS HOME SO WE CAN TAKE HER WITH US RIGHT AWAY.
LOOK! HERE COME TWO POLICEMEN!
WHAT LUCK! POLICEMEN ARE MY SECOND FAVORITE THING, AFTER RHUBARB PUDDING.
ARE YOU THE LITTLE GIRL WHO HAS MOVED INTO VILLA VILLEKULLA?
NOPE. I'M A LITTLE OLD WOMAN WHO LIVES ON THE OTHER SIDE OF TOWN.
DON'T BE FUNNY. TELL US YOUR NAME.
PIPPILOTTA VICTUALIA WINDOWSHADE CURLYMINT EPHRAIMSDAUGHTER LONGSTOCKING.
MY DEAR PIPPI LONGSTOCKING. WE'RE SUPPOSED TO TAKE YOU TO A CHILDREN'S HOME.
BUT I ALREADY HAVE ONE. I'M A CHILD AND THIS IS MY HOME. SO THIS IS A CHILDREN'S HOME.

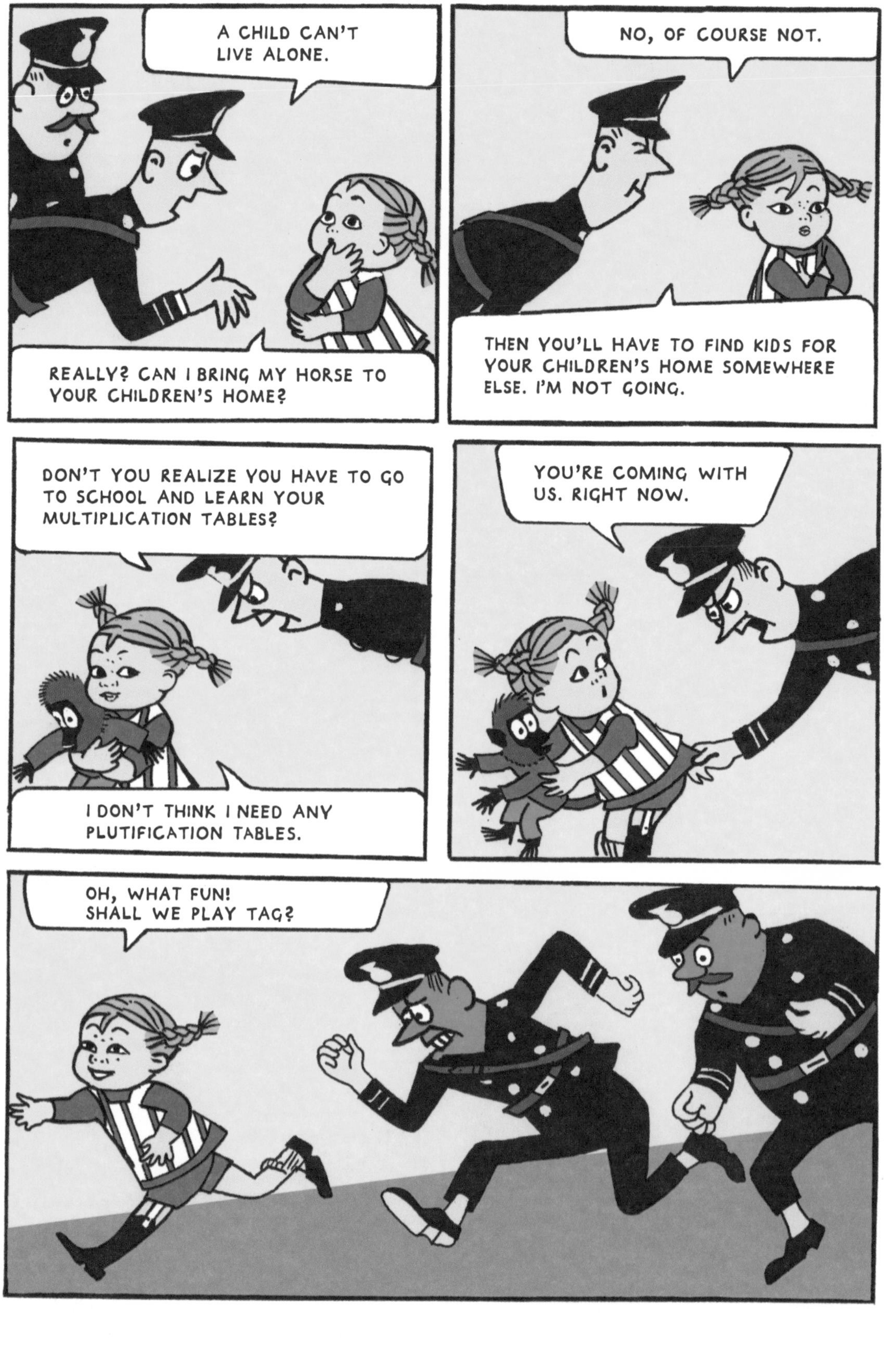
A CHILD CAN'T LIVE ALONE.
REALLY? CAN I BRING MY HORSE TO YOUR CHILDREN'S HOME?
NO, OF COURSE NOT.
THEN YOU'LL HAVE TO FIND KIDS FOR YOUR CHILDREN'S HOME SOMEWHERE ELSE. I'M NOT GOING.
DON'T YOU REALIZE YOU HAVE TO GO TO SCHOOL AND LEARN YOUR MULTIPLICATION TABLES?
I DON'T THINK I NEED ANY PLUTIFICATION TABLES.
YOU'RE COMING WITH US. RIGHT NOW.
OH, WHAT FUN! SHALL WE PLAY TAG?

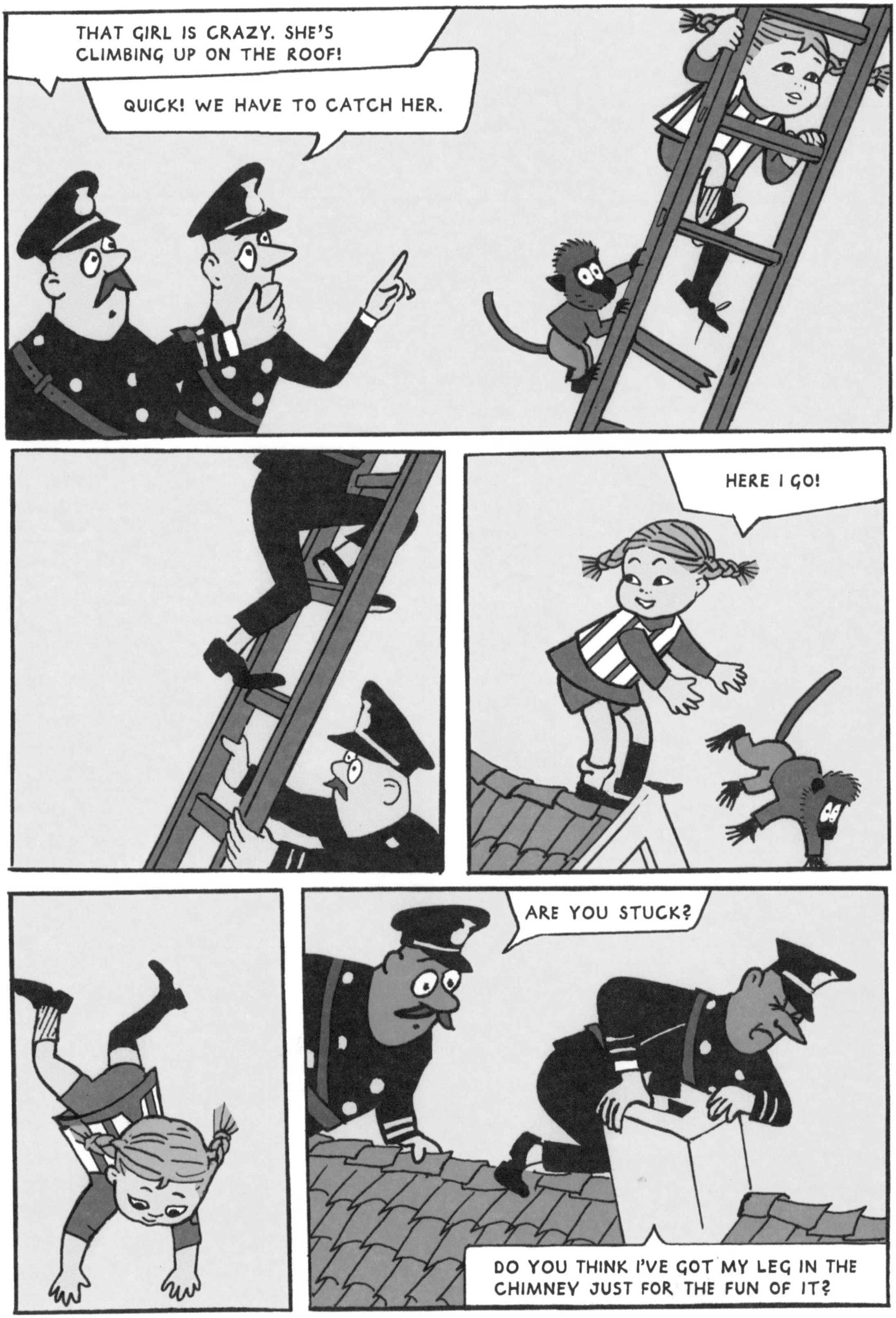
THAT GIRL IS CRAZY. SHE'S CLIMBING UP ON THE ROOF!
QUICK! WE HAVE TO CATCH HER.
HERE I GO!
ARE YOU STUCK?
DO YOU THINK I'VE GOT MY LEG IN THE CHIMNEY JUST FOR THE FUN OF IT?

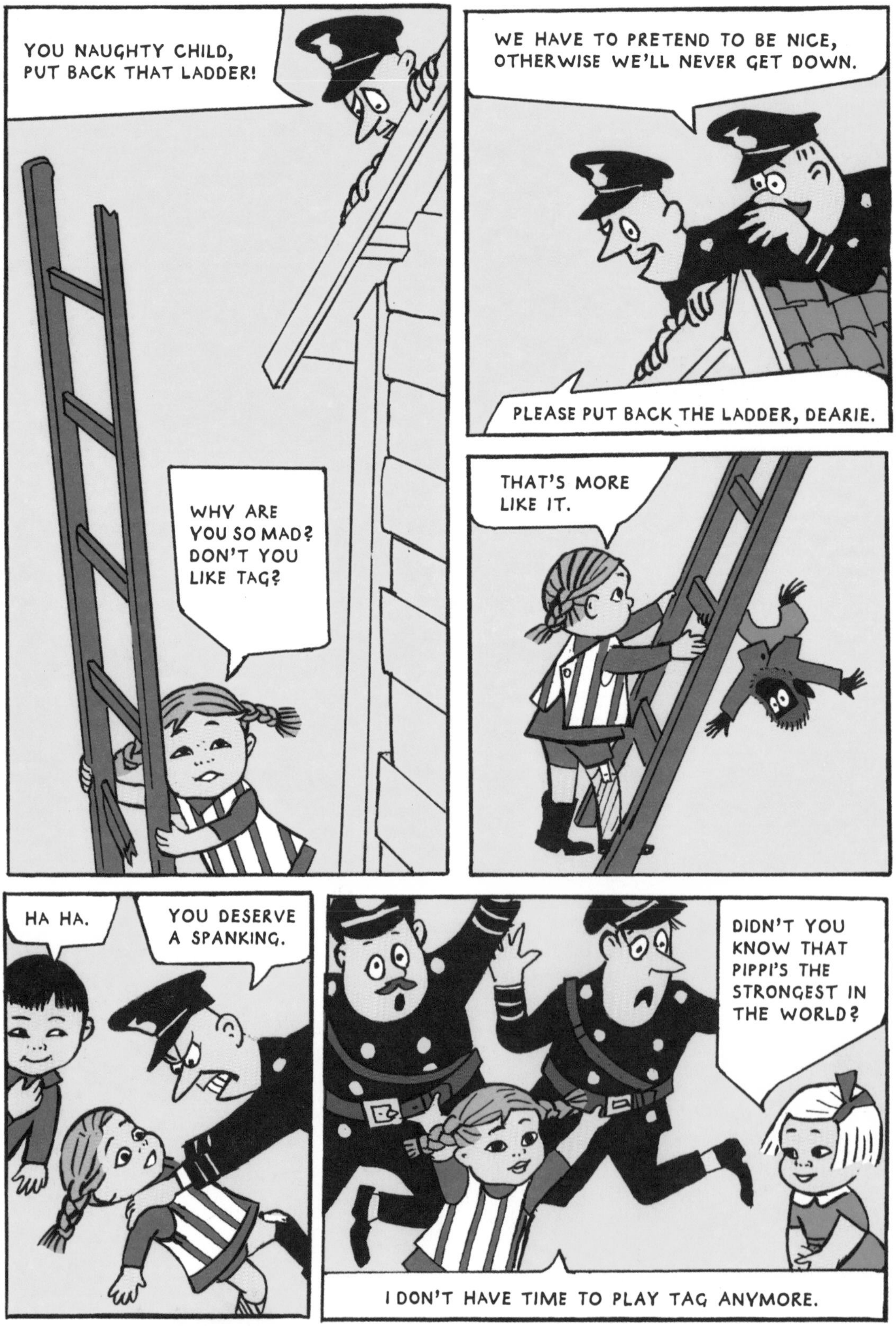
YOU NAUGHTY CHILD, PUT BACK THAT LADDER!
WHY ARE YOU SO MAD? DON'T YOU LIKE TAG?
WE HAVE TO PRETEND TO BE NICE, OTHERWISE WE'LL NEVER GET DOWN.
PLEASE PUT BACK THE LADDER, DEARIE.
THAT'S MORE LIKE IT.
HA HA.
YOU DESERVE A SPANKING.
DIDN'T YOU KNOW THAT PIPPI'S THE STRONGEST IN THE WORLD?
I DON'T HAVE TIME TO PLAY TAG ANYMORE.

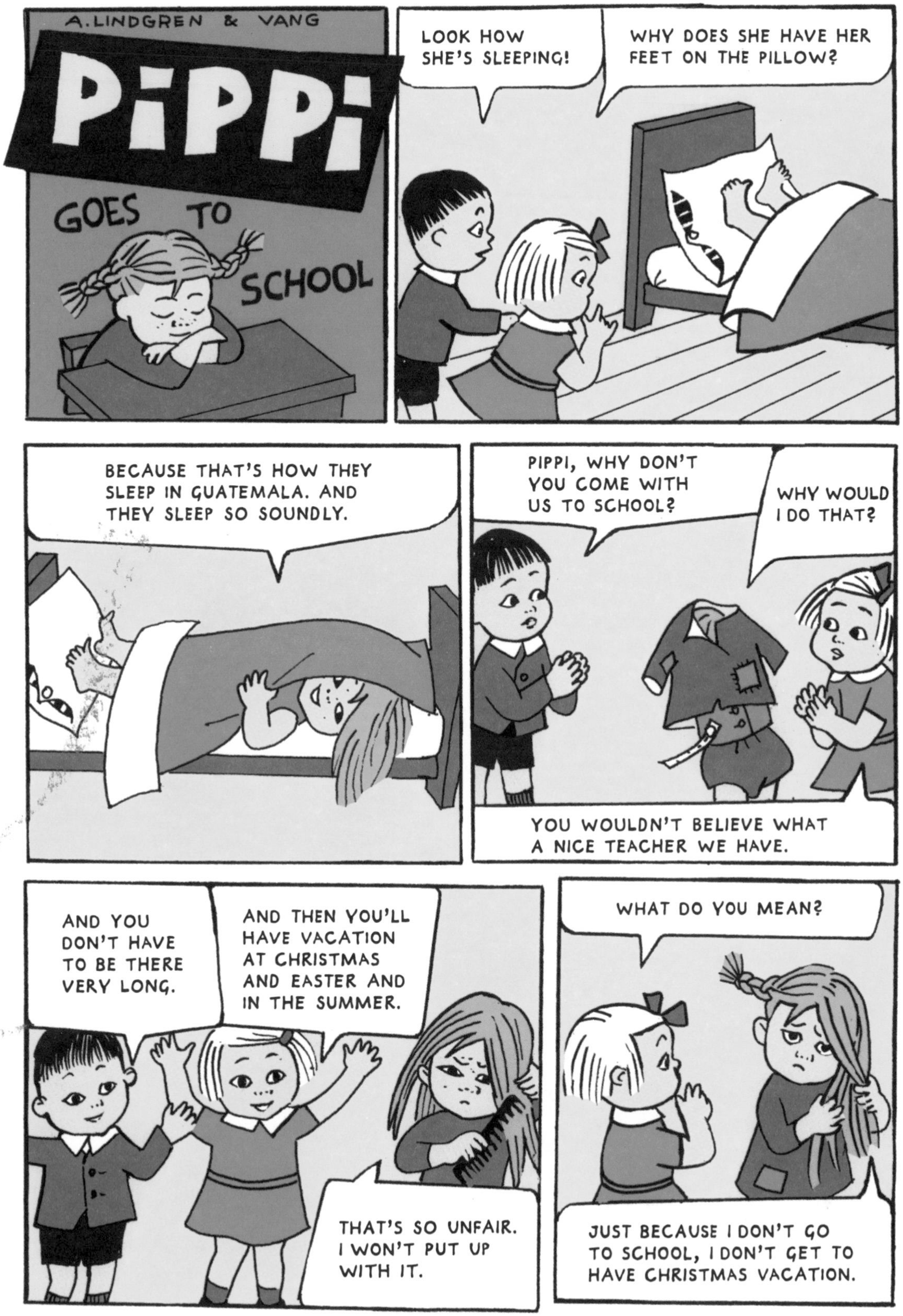
A. LINDGREN & VANG
PIPPI
GOES TO SCHOOL
LOOK HOW SHE'S SLEEPING!
WHY DOES SHE HAVE HER FEET ON THE PILLOW?
BECAUSE THAT'S HOW THEY SLEEP IN GUATEMALA. AND THEY SLEEP SO SOUNDLY.
PIPPI, WHY DON'T YOU COME WITH US TO SCHOOL?
WHY WOULD I DO THAT?
YOU WOULDN'T BELIEVE WHAT A NICE TEACHER WE HAVE.
AND YOU DON'T HAVE TO BE THERE VERY LONG.
AND THEN YOU'LL HAVE VACATION AT CHRISTMAS AND EASTER AND IN THE SUMMER.
THAT'S SO UNFAIR. I WON'T PUT UP WITH IT.
WHAT DO YOU MEAN?
JUST BECAUSE I DON'T GO TO SCHOOL, I DON'T GET TO HAVE CHRISTMAS VACATION.

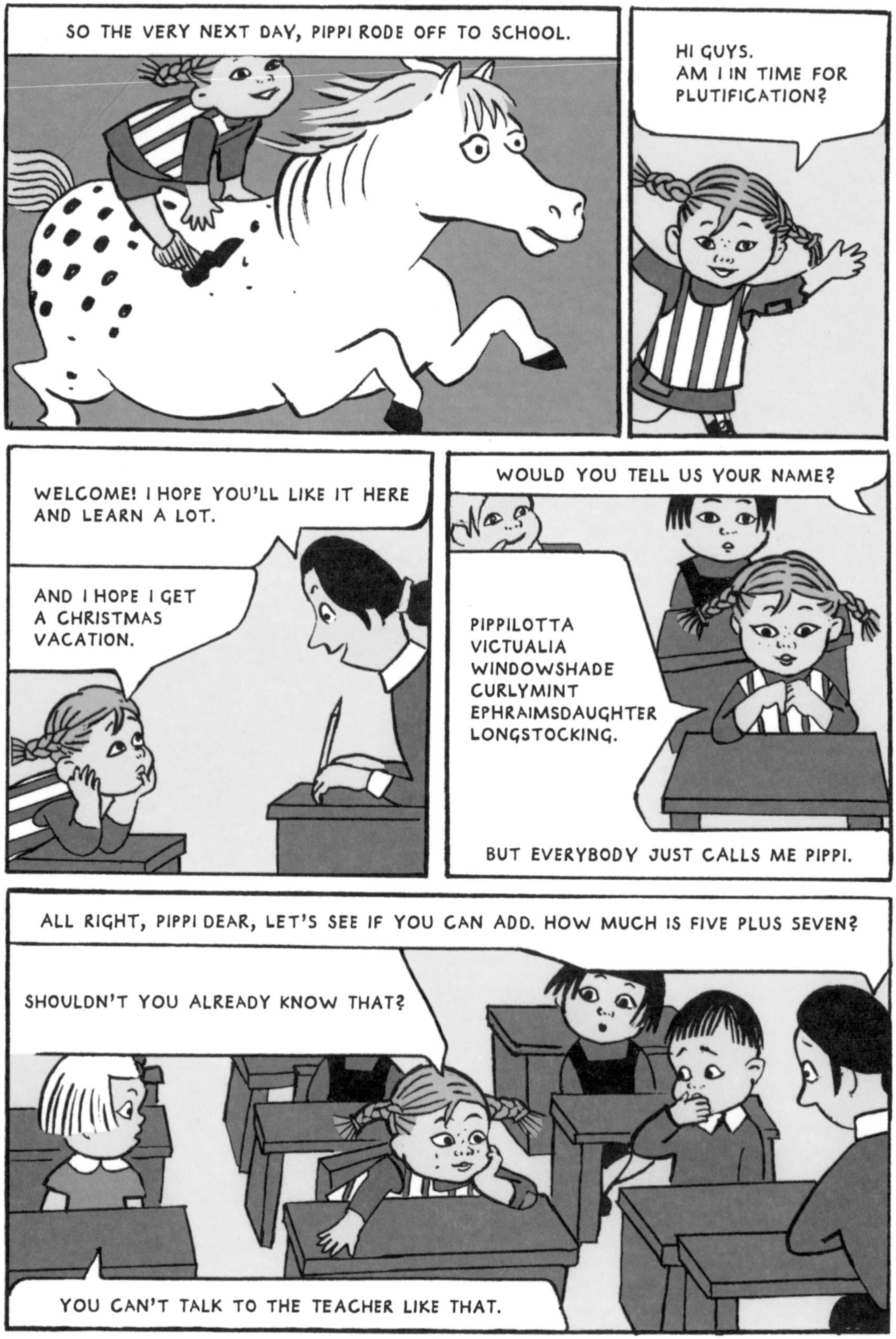
SO THE VERY NEXT DAY, PIPPI RODE OFF TO SCHOOL.
HI GUYS. AM I IN TIME FOR PLUTIFICATION?
WELCOME! I HOPE YOU'LL LIKE IT HERE AND LEARN A LOT.
AND I HOPE I GET A CHRISTMAS VACATION.
WOULD YOU TELL US YOUR NAME?
PIPPILOTTA VICTUALIA WINDOWSHADE CURLYMINT EPHRAIMSDAUGHTER LONGSTOCKING.
BUT EVERYBODY JUST CALLS ME PIPPI.
ALL RIGHT, PIPPI DEAR, LET'S SEE IF YOU CAN ADD. HOW MUCH IS FIVE PLUS SEVEN?
SHOULDN'T YOU ALREADY KNOW THAT?
YOU CAN'T TALK TO THE TEACHER LIKE THAT.

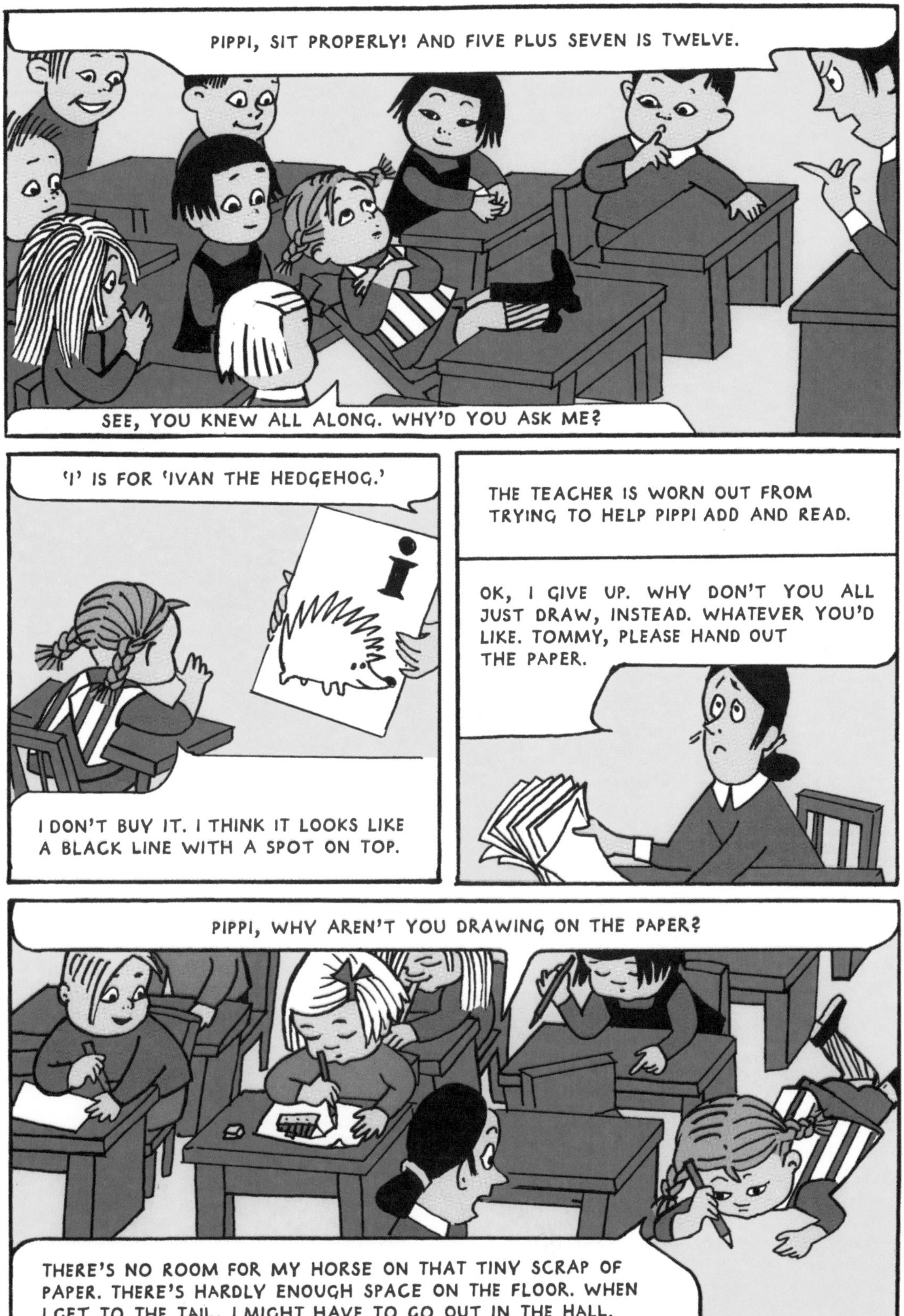
PIPPI, SIT PROPERLY! AND FIVE PLUS SEVEN IS TWELVE.
SEE, YOU KNEW ALL ALONG. WHY'D YOU ASK ME?
'I' IS FOR 'IVAN THE HEDGEHOG.'
i
I DON'T BUY IT. I THINK IT LOOKS LIKE A BLACK LINE WITH A SPOT ON TOP.
THE TEACHER IS WORN OUT FROM TRYING TO HELP PIPPI ADD AND READ.
OK, I GIVE UP. WHY DON'T YOU ALL JUST DRAW, INSTEAD. WHATEVER YOU'D LIKE. TOMMY, PLEASE HAND OUT THE PAPER.
PIPPI, WHY AREN'T YOU DRAWING ON THE PAPER?
THERE'S NO ROOM FOR MY HORSE ON THAT TINY SCRAP OF PAPER. THERE'S HARDLY ENOUGH SPACE ON THE FLOOR. WHEN I GET TO THE TAIL, I MIGHT HAVE TO GO OUT IN THE HALL.

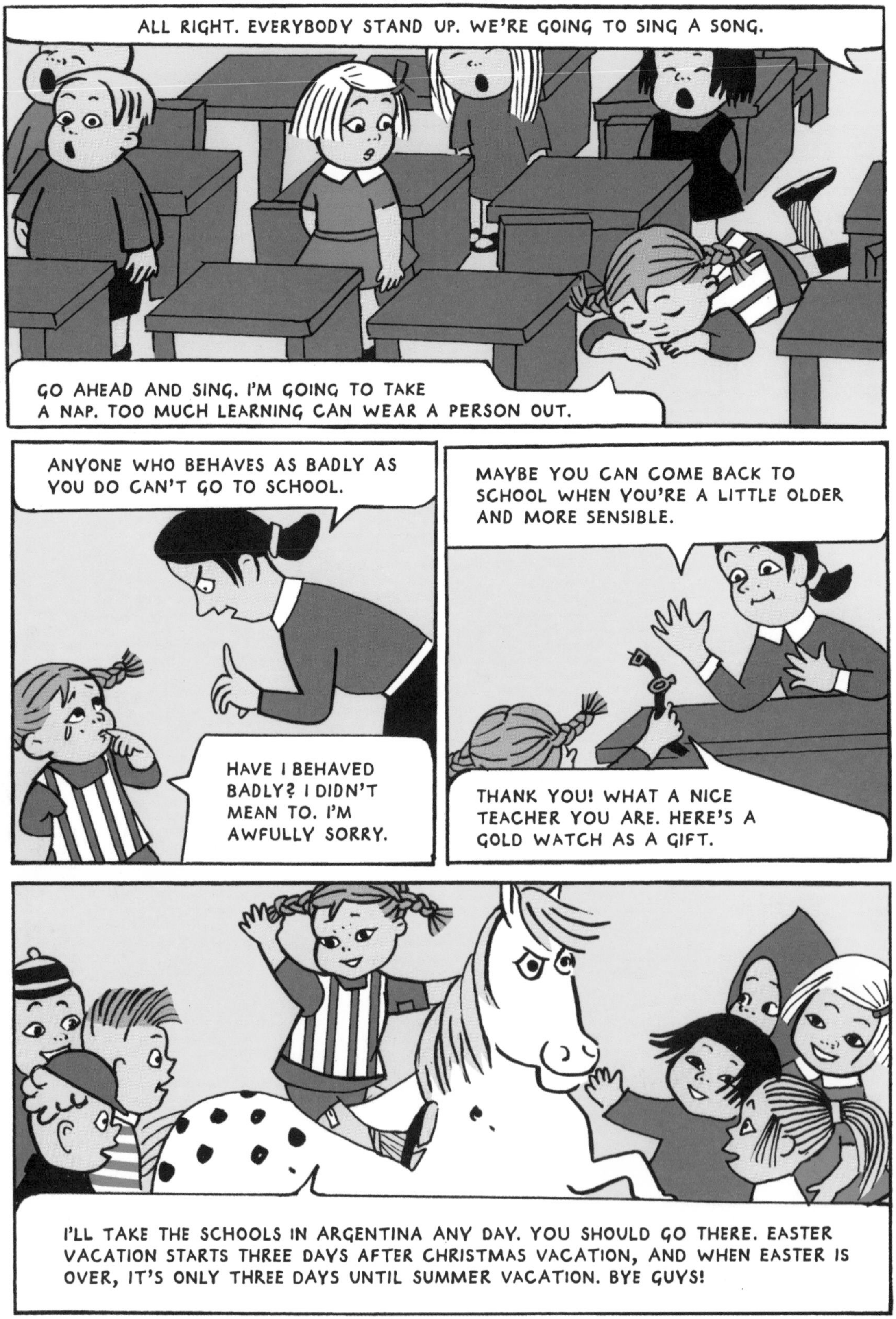
ALL RIGHT. EVERYBODY STAND UP. WE'RE GOING TO SING A SONG.
GO AHEAD AND SING. I'M GOING TO TAKE A NAP. TOO MUCH LEARNING CAN WEAR A PERSON OUT.
ANYONE WHO BEHAVES AS BADLY AS YOU DO CAN'T GO TO SCHOOL.
HAVE I BEHAVED BADLY? I DIDN'T MEAN TO. I'M AWFULLY SORRY.
MAYBE YOU CAN COME BACK TO SCHOOL WHEN YOU'RE A LITTLE OLDER AND MORE SENSIBLE.
THANK YOU! WHAT A NICE TEACHER YOU ARE. HERE'S A GOLD WATCH AS A GIFT.
I'LL TAKE THE SCHOOLS IN ARGENTINA ANY DAY. YOU SHOULD GO THERE. EASTER VACATION STARTS THREE DAYS AFTER CHRISTMAS VACATION, AND WHEN EASTER IS OVER, IT'S ONLY THREE DAYS UNTIL SUMMER VACATION. BYE GUYS!

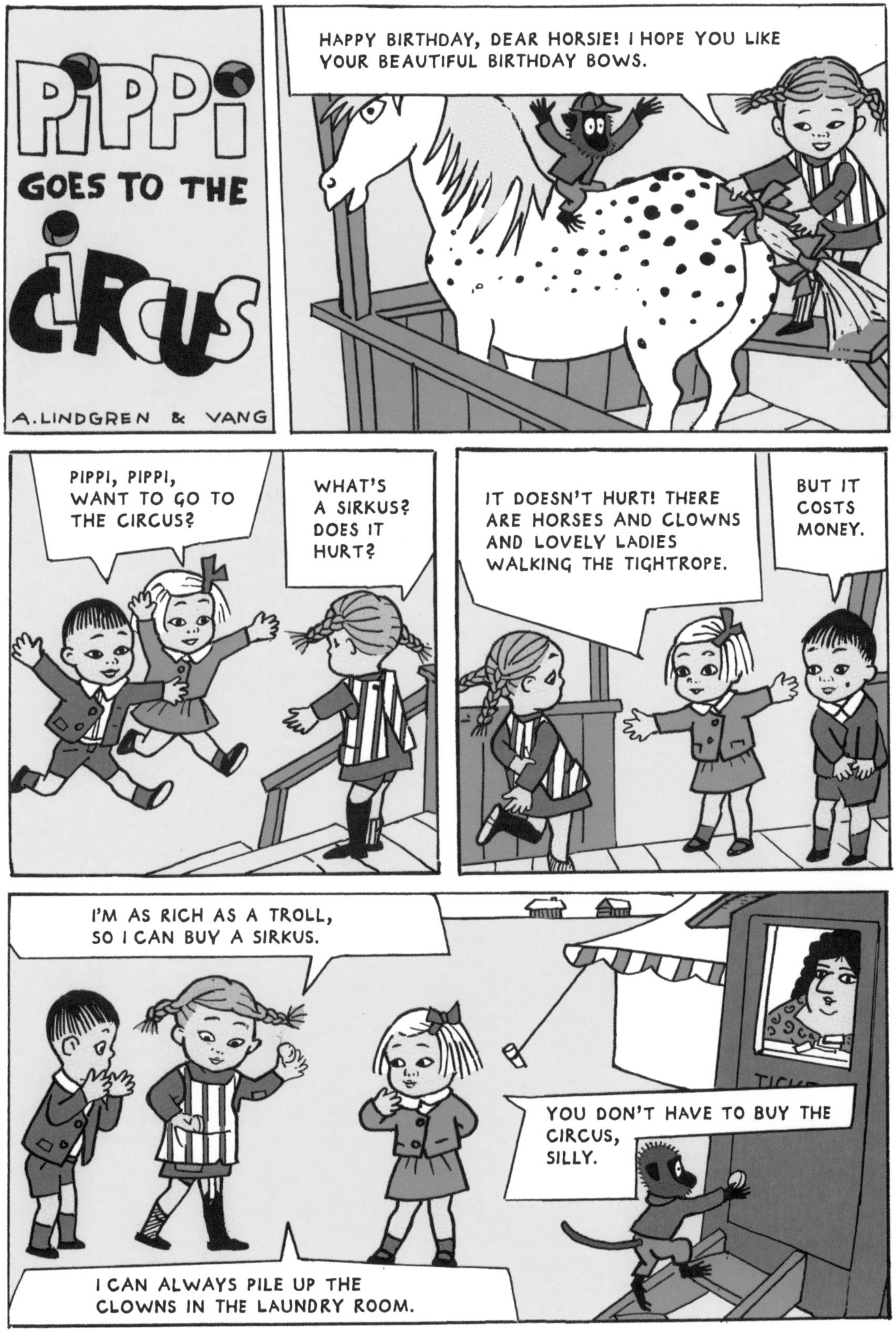
PIPPI GOES TO THE CIRCUS
A. LINDGREN & VANG
HAPPY BIRTHDAY, DEAR HORSIE! I HOPE YOU LIKE YOUR BEAUTIFUL BIRTHDAY BOWS.
PIPPI, PIPPI, WANT TO GO TO THE CIRCUS?
WHAT'S A SIRKUS? DOES IT HURT?
IT DOESN'T HURT! THERE ARE HORSES AND CLOWNS AND LOVELY LADIES WALKING THE TIGHTROPE.
BUT IT COSTS MONEY.
I'M AS RICH AS A TROLL, SO I CAN BUY A SIRKUS.
YOU DON'T HAVE TO BUY THE CIRCUS, SILLY.
I CAN ALWAYS PILE UP THE CLOWNS IN THE LAUNDRY ROOM.

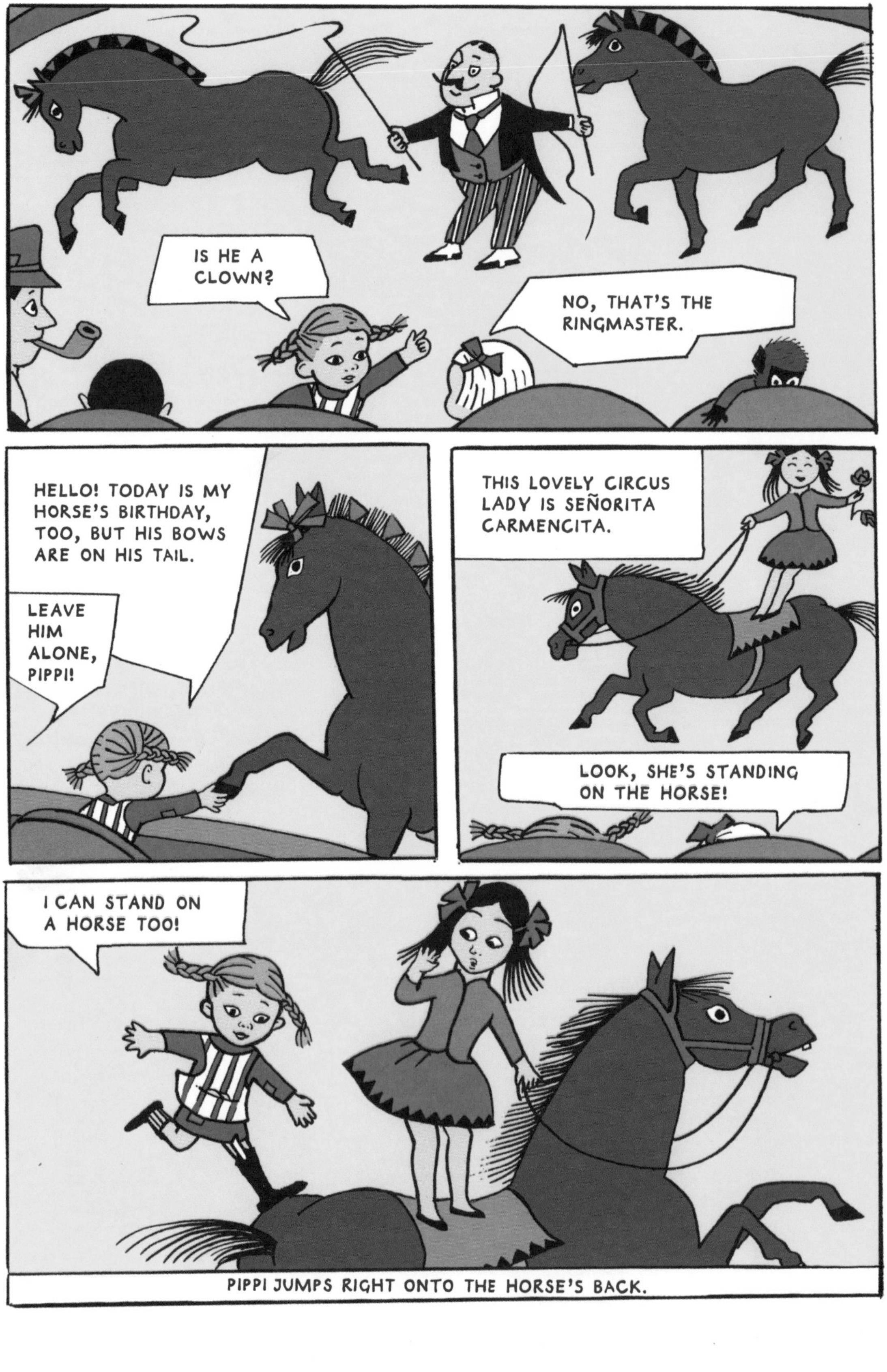

IS HE A CLOWN?
NO, THAT'S THE RINGMASTER.
HELLO! TODAY IS MY HORSE'S BIRTHDAY, TOO, BUT HIS BOWS ARE ON HIS TAIL.
LEAVE HIM ALONE, PIPPI!
THIS LOVELY CIRCUS LADY IS SEÑORITA CARMENCITA.
LOOK, SHE'S STANDING ON THE HORSE!
I CAN STAND ON A HORSE TOO!

PIPPI JUMPS RIGHT ONTO THE HORSE'S BACK.

GET OFF, YOU NAUGHTY GIRL!

SIMMER DOWN! YOU'RE NOT THE ONLY ONE ALLOWED TO HAVE FUN.

IT'S OK, I CAN RIDE AGAIN ANOTHER DAY.

THE RINGMASTER SENT TWO MEN OVER TO THROW PIPPI OUT—BUT THEY COULDN'T BUDGE HER.

YOU MIGHT AS WELL GIVE UP. YOU'LL JUST RUIN YOUR NAILS.

HERE IS MISS ELVIRA, TIGHTROPE WALKER!

WALK THE TIGHTROPE? I CAN DO THAT, TOO.

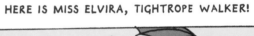

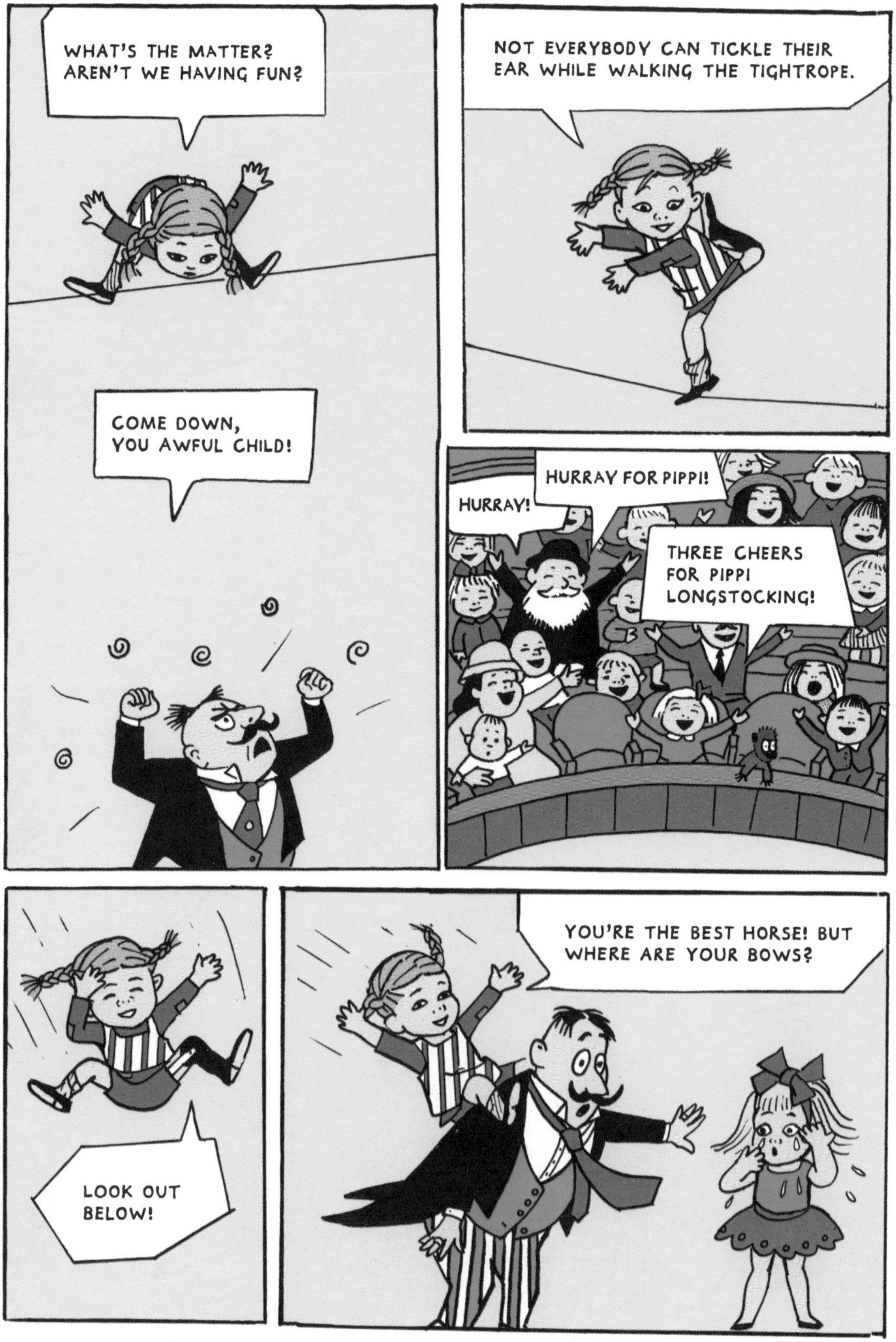
WHAT'S THE MATTER? AREN'T WE HAVING FUN?
NOT EVERYBODY CAN TICKLE THEIR EAR WHILE WALKING THE TIGHTROPE.
COME DOWN, YOU AWFUL CHILD!
HURRAY!
HURRAY FOR PIPPI!
THREE CHEERS FOR PIPPI LONGSTOCKING!
LOOK OUT BELOW!
YOU'RE THE BEST HORSE! BUT WHERE ARE YOUR BOWS?

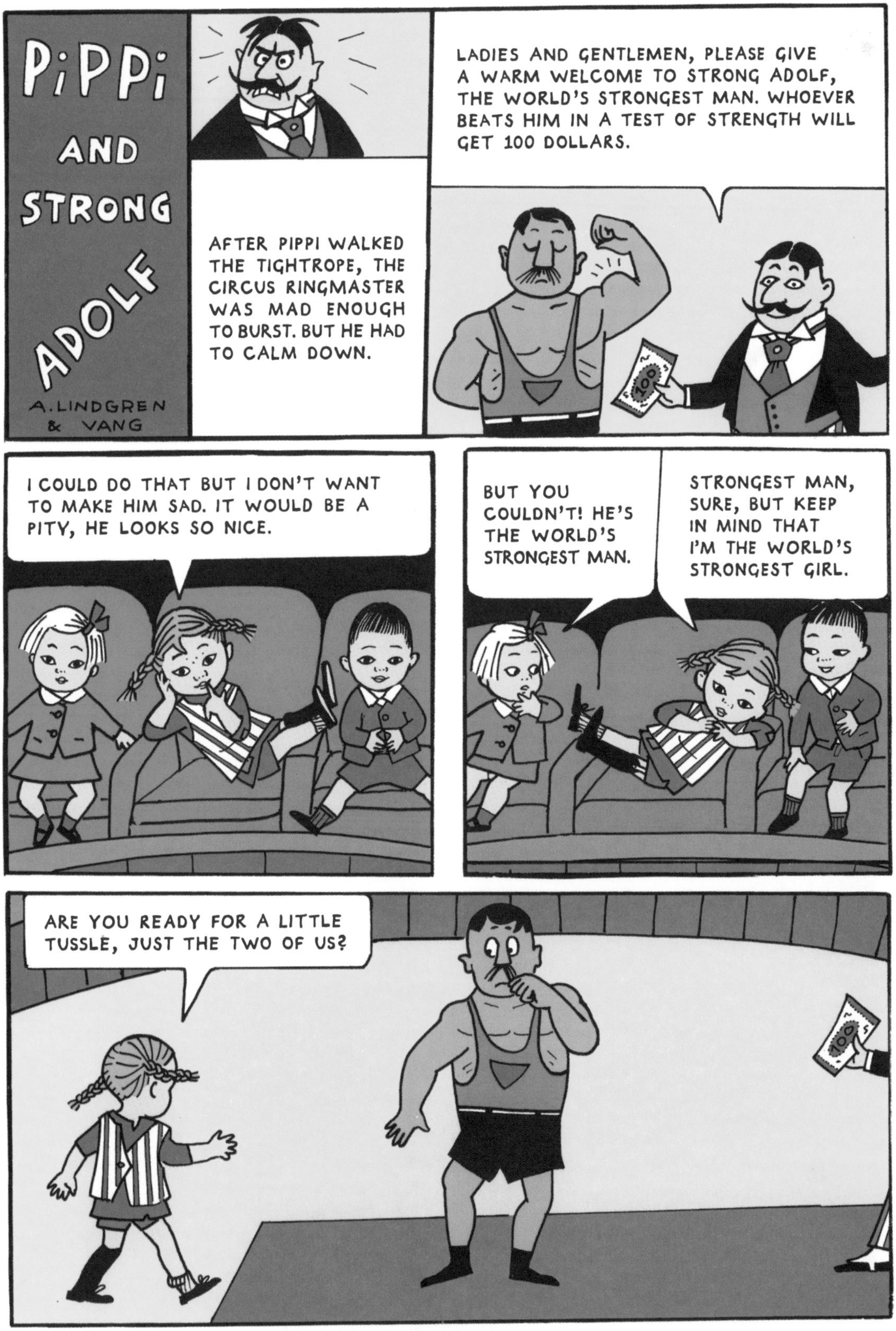

PIPPI AND STRONG ADOLF
A. LINDGREN & VANG
AFTER PIPPI WALKED THE TIGHTROPE, THE CIRCUS RINGMASTER WAS MAD ENOUGH TO BURST. BUT HE HAD TO CALM DOWN.
LADIES AND GENTLEMEN, PLEASE GIVE A WARM WELCOME TO STRONG ADOLF, THE WORLD'S STRONGEST MAN. WHOEVER BEATS HIM IN A TEST OF STRENGTH WILL GET 100 DOLLARS.
100
I COULD DO THAT BUT I DON'T WANT TO MAKE HIM SAD. IT WOULD BE A PITY, HE LOOKS SO NICE.
BUT YOU COULDN'T! HE'S THE WORLD'S STRONGEST MAN.
STRONGEST MAN, SURE, BUT KEEP IN MIND THAT I'M THE WORLD'S STRONGEST GIRL.
ARE YOU READY FOR A LITTLE TUSSLE, JUST THE TWO OF US?
100

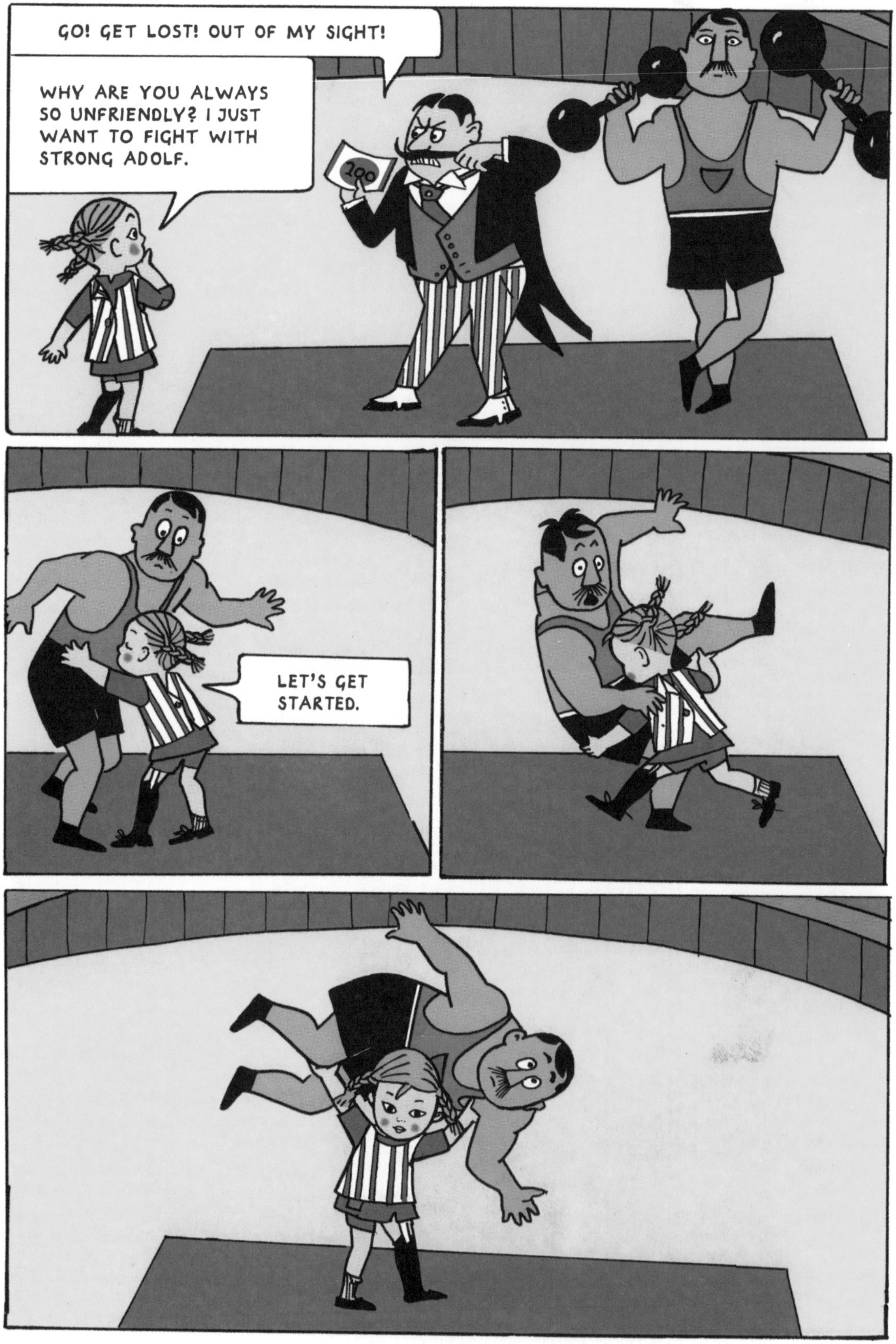
GO! GET LOST! OUT OF MY SIGHT!
WHY ARE YOU ALWAYS SO UNFRIENDLY? I JUST WANT TO FIGHT WITH STRONG ADOLF.
200
LET'S GET STARTED.

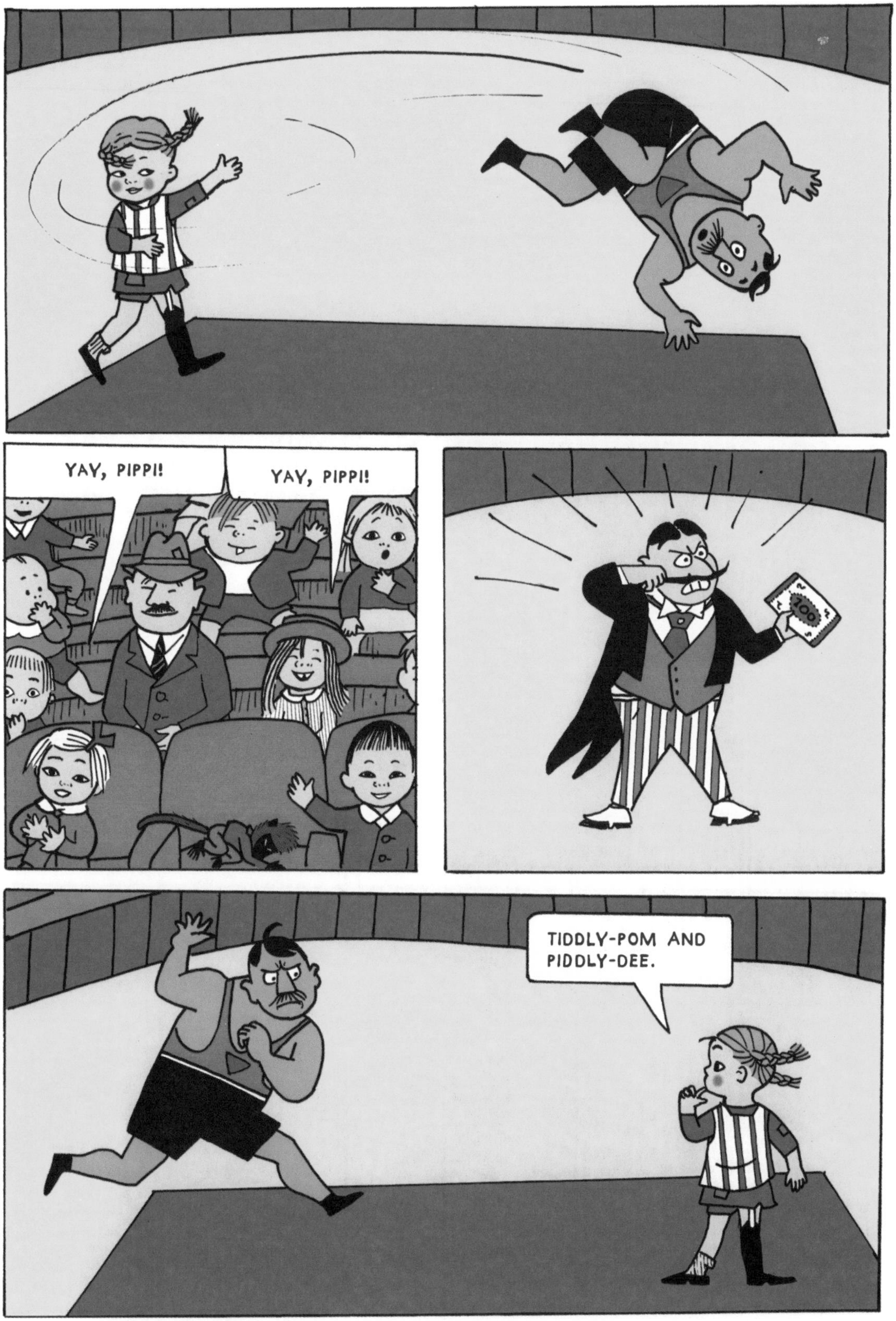
YAY, PIPPI!
YAY, PIPPI!
ZOO
TIDDLY-POM AND PIDDLY-DEE.

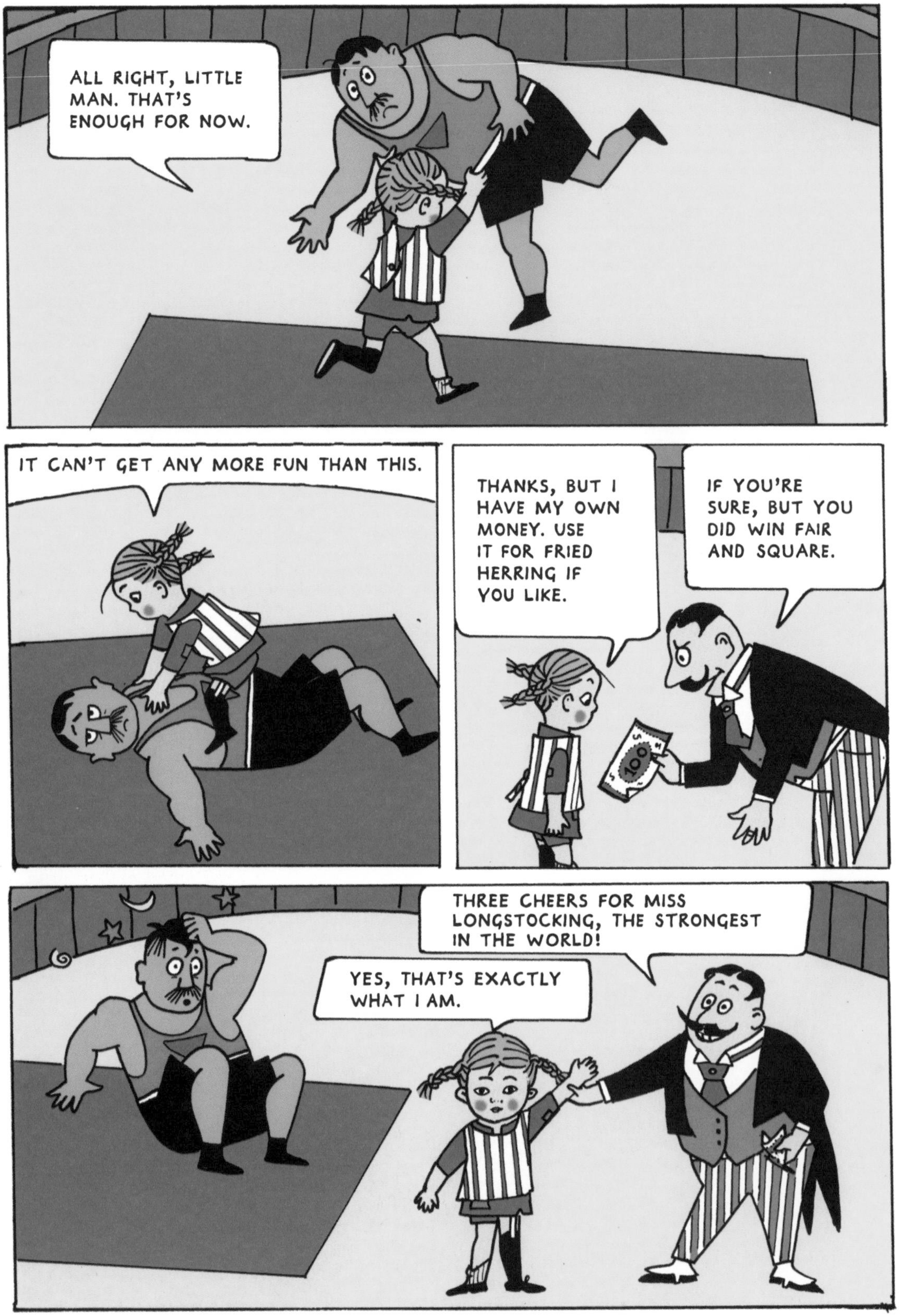
ALL RIGHT, LITTLE MAN. THAT'S ENOUGH FOR NOW.
IT CAN'T GET ANY MORE FUN THAN THIS.
THANKS, BUT I HAVE MY OWN MONEY. USE IT FOR FRIED HERRING IF YOU LIKE.
IF YOU'RE SURE, BUT YOU DID WIN FAIR AND SQUARE.
100
THREE CHEERS FOR MISS LONGSTOCKING, THE STRONGEST IN THE WORLD!
YES, THAT'S EXACTLY WHAT I AM.

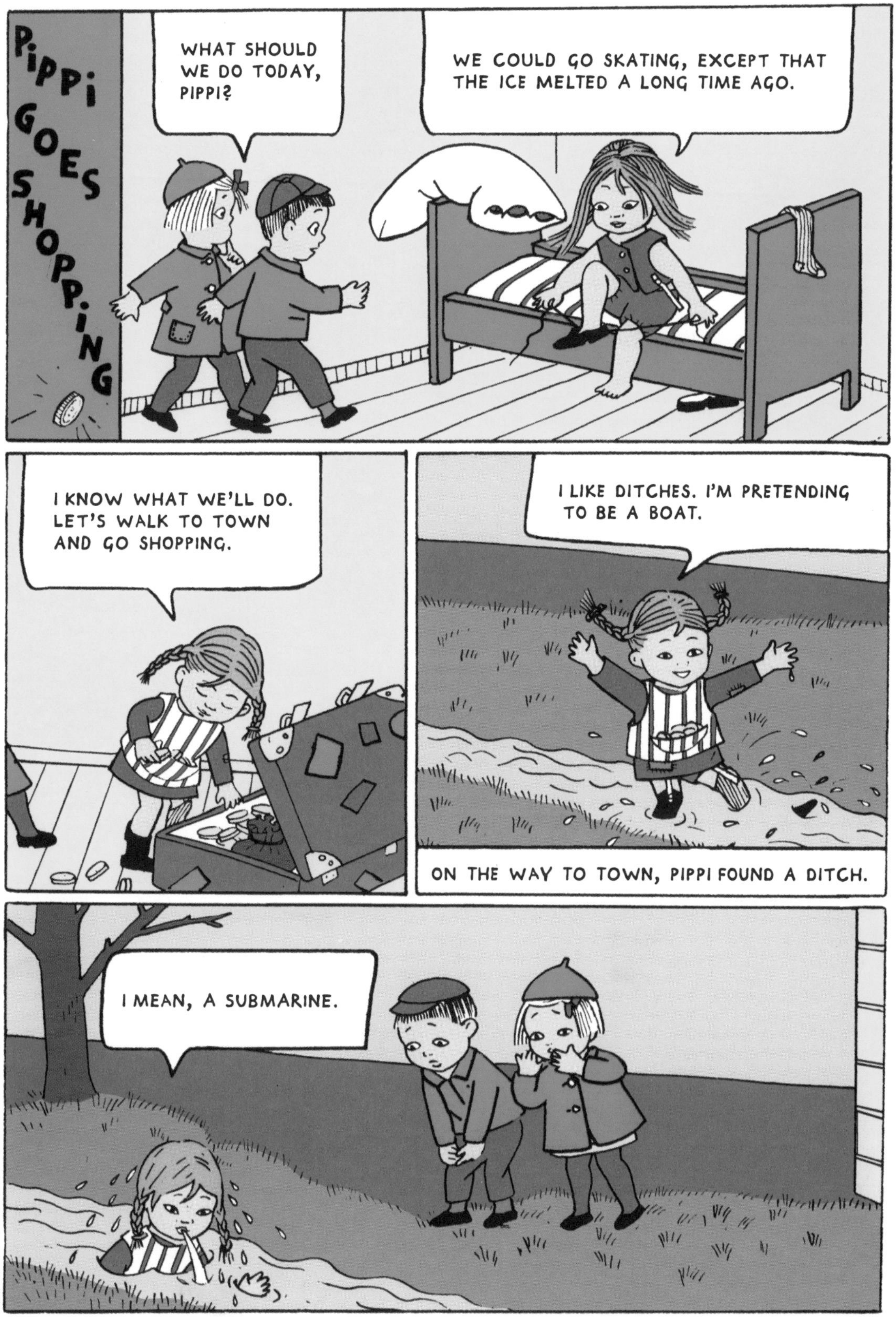
PIPPI GOES SHOPPING
WHAT SHOULD WE DO TODAY, PIPPI?
WE COULD GO SKATING, EXCEPT THAT THE ICE MELTED A LONG TIME AGO.
I KNOW WHAT WE'LL DO. LET'S WALK TO TOWN AND GO SHOPPING.
I LIKE DITCHES. I'M PRETENDING TO BE A BOAT.
ON THE WAY TO TOWN, PIPPI FOUND A DITCH.
I MEAN, A SUBMARINE.

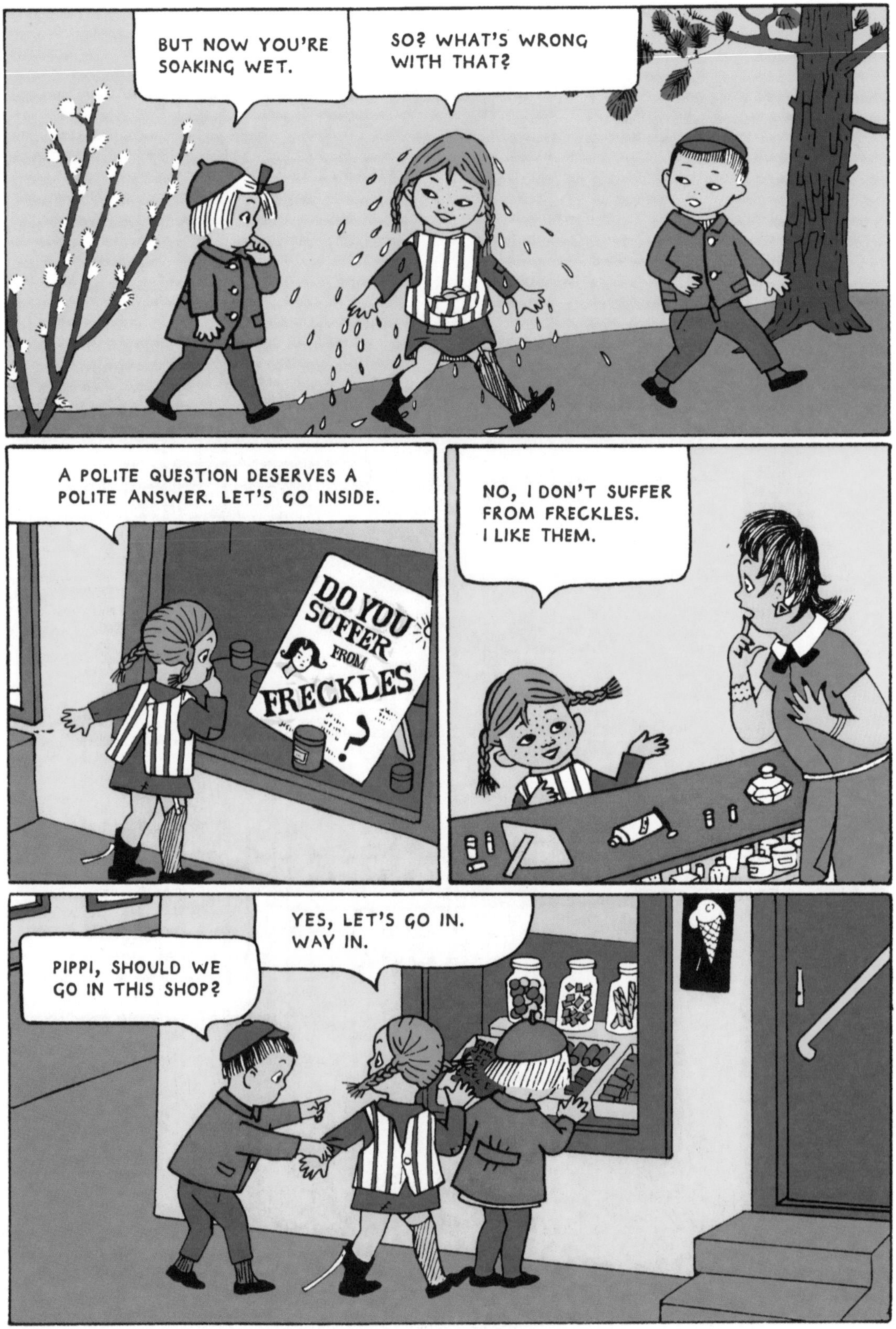
BUT NOW YOU'RE SOAKING WET.
SO? WHAT'S WRONG WITH THAT?
A POLITE QUESTION DESERVES A POLITE ANSWER. LET'S GO INSIDE.
DO YOU SUFFER FROM FRECKLES ?
NO, I DON'T SUFFER FROM FRECKLES. I LIKE THEM.
PIPPI, SHOULD WE GO IN THIS SHOP?
YES, LET'S GO IN. WAY IN.

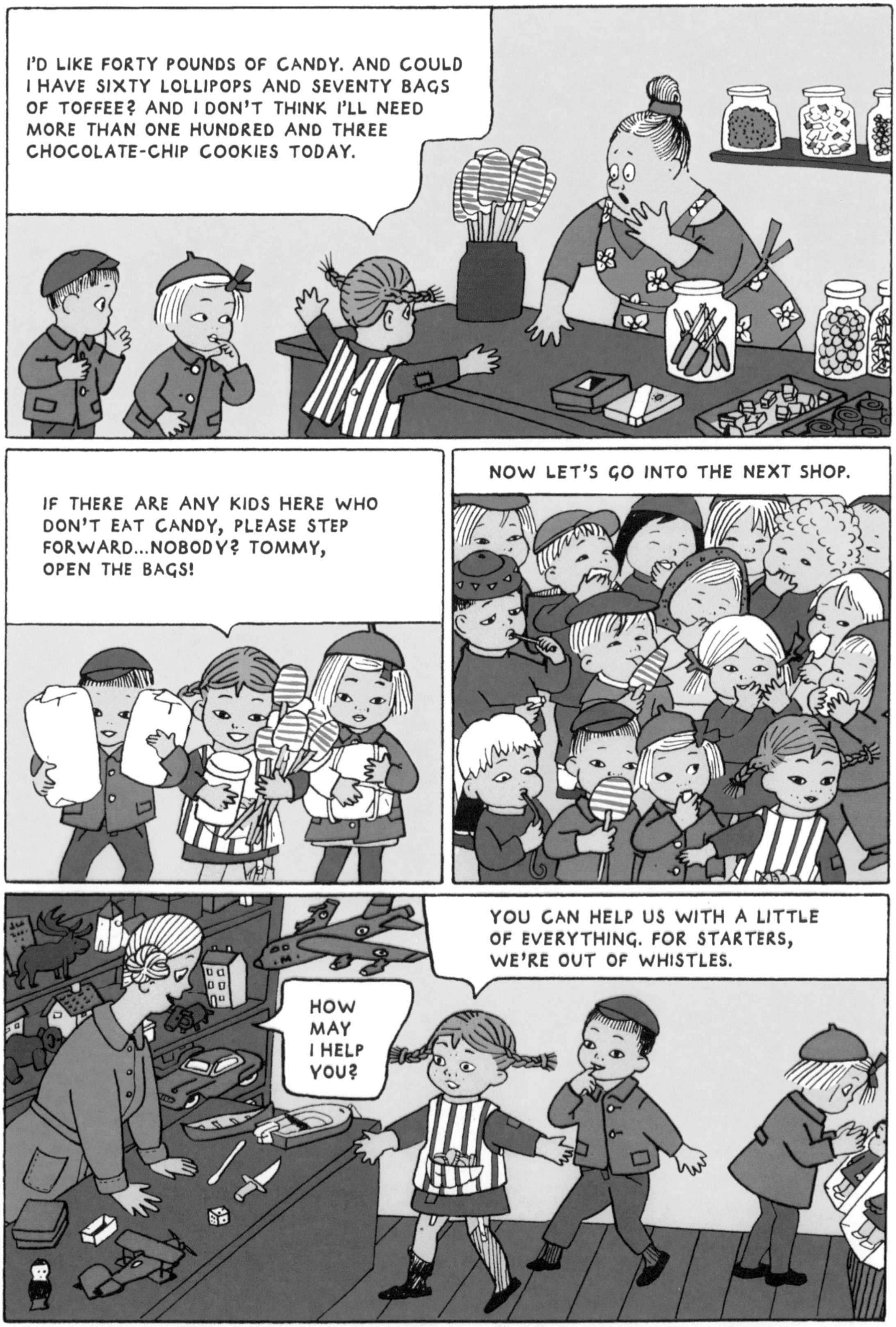

I'D LIKE FORTY POUNDS OF CANDY. AND COULD I HAVE SIXTY LOLLIPOPS AND SEVENTY BAGS OF TOFFEE? AND I DON'T THINK I'LL NEED MORE THAN ONE HUNDRED AND THREE CHOCOLATE-CHIP COOKIES TODAY.
IF THERE ARE ANY KIDS HERE WHO DON'T EAT CANDY, PLEASE STEP FORWARD...NOBODY? TOMMY, OPEN THE BAGS!
NOW LET'S GO INTO THE NEXT SHOP.
HOW MAY I HELP YOU?
YOU CAN HELP US WITH A LITTLE OF EVERYTHING. FOR STARTERS, WE'RE OUT OF WHISTLES.

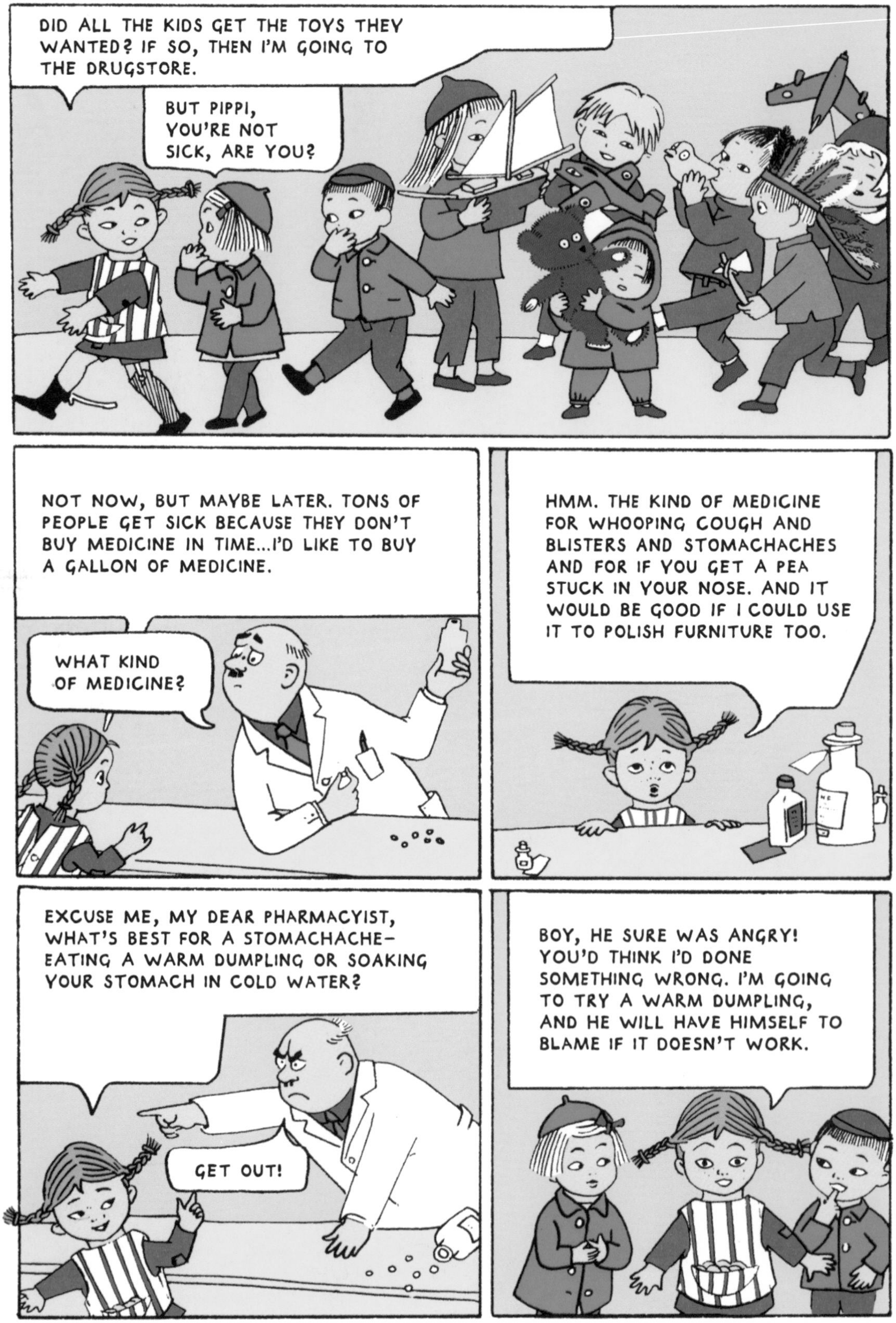
DID ALL THE KIDS GET THE TOYS THEY WANTED? IF SO, THEN I'M GOING TO THE DRUGSTORE.
BUT PIPPI, YOU'RE NOT SICK, ARE YOU?
NOT NOW, BUT MAYBE LATER. TONS OF PEOPLE GET SICK BECAUSE THEY DON'T BUY MEDICINE IN TIME...I'D LIKE TO BUY A GALLON OF MEDICINE.
WHAT KIND OF MEDICINE?
HMM. THE KIND OF MEDICINE FOR WHOOPING COUGH AND BLISTERS AND STOMACHACHES AND FOR IF YOU GET A PEA STUCK IN YOUR NOSE. AND IT WOULD BE GOOD IF I COULD USE IT TO POLISH FURNITURE TOO.
EXCUSE ME, MY DEAR PHARMACYIST, WHAT'S BEST FOR A STOMACHACHE— EATING A WARM DUMPLING OR SOAKING YOUR STOMACH IN COLD WATER?
GET OUT!
BOY, HE SURE WAS ANGRY! YOU'D THINK I'D DONE SOMETHING WRONG. I'M GOING TO TRY A WARM DUMPLING, AND HE WILL HAVE HIMSELF TO BLAME IF IT DOESN'T WORK.

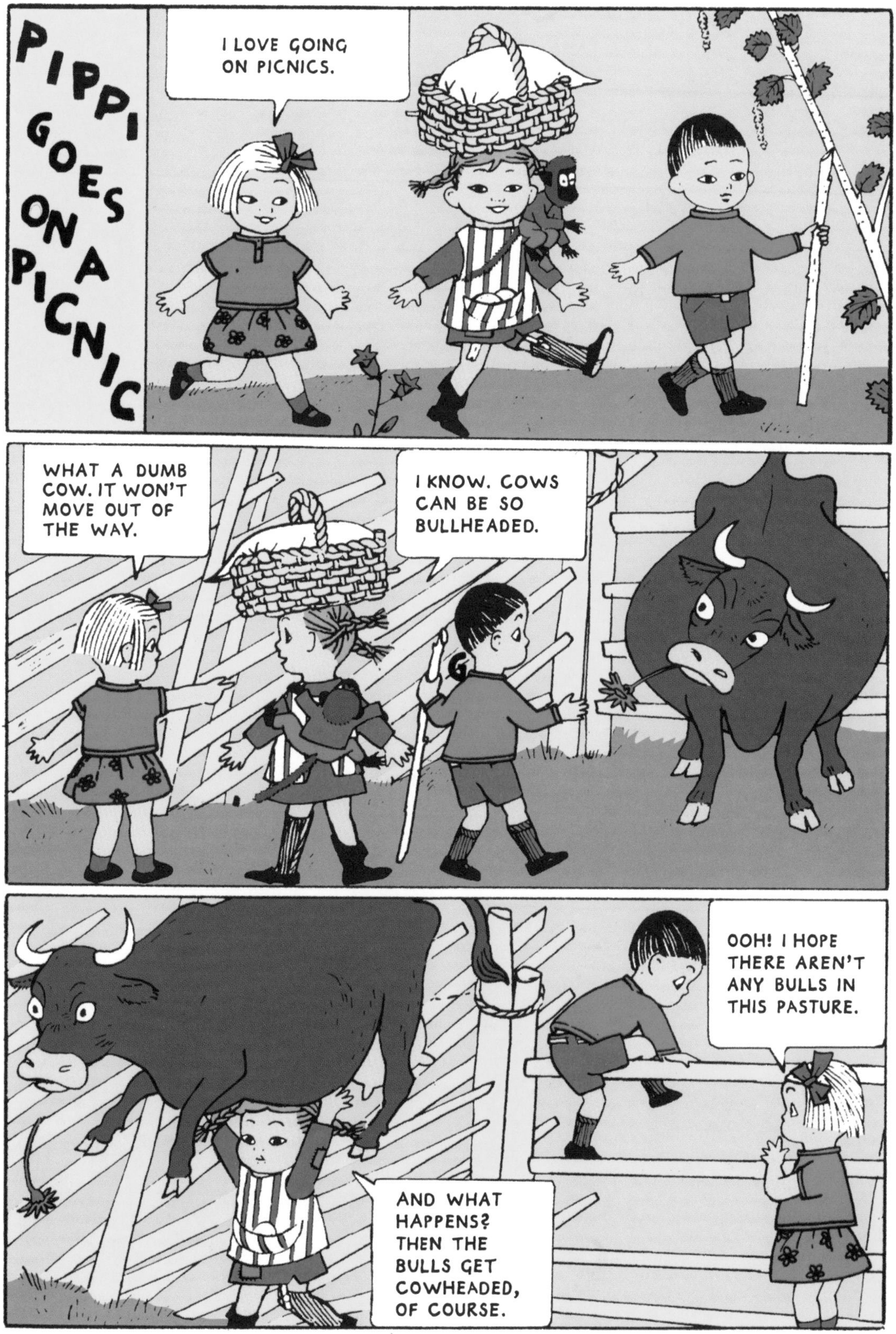
PIPPI GOES ON A PICNIC
I LOVE GOING ON PICNICS.
WHAT A DUMB COW. IT WON'T MOVE OUT OF THE WAY.
I KNOW. COWS CAN BE SO BULLHEADED.
OOH! I HOPE THERE AREN'T ANY BULLS IN THIS PASTURE.
AND WHAT HAPPENS? THEN THE BULLS GET COWHEADED, OF COURSE.

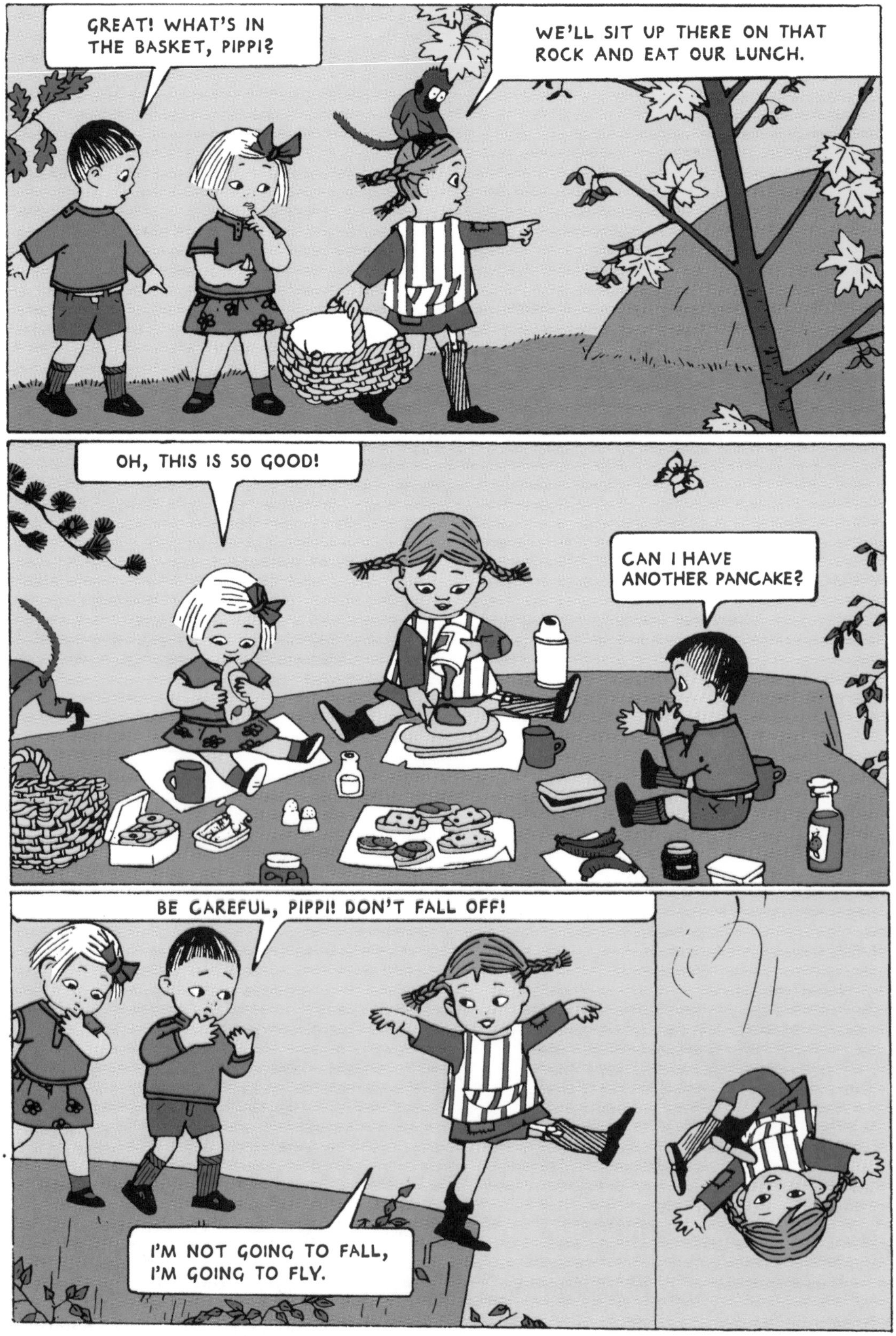
GREAT! WHAT'S IN THE BASKET, PIPPI?
WE'LL SIT UP THERE ON THAT ROCK AND EAT OUR LUNCH.
OH, THIS IS SO GOOD!
CAN I HAVE ANOTHER PANCAKE?
BE CAREFUL, PIPPI! DON'T FALL OFF!
I'M NOT GOING TO FALL, I'M GOING TO FLY.

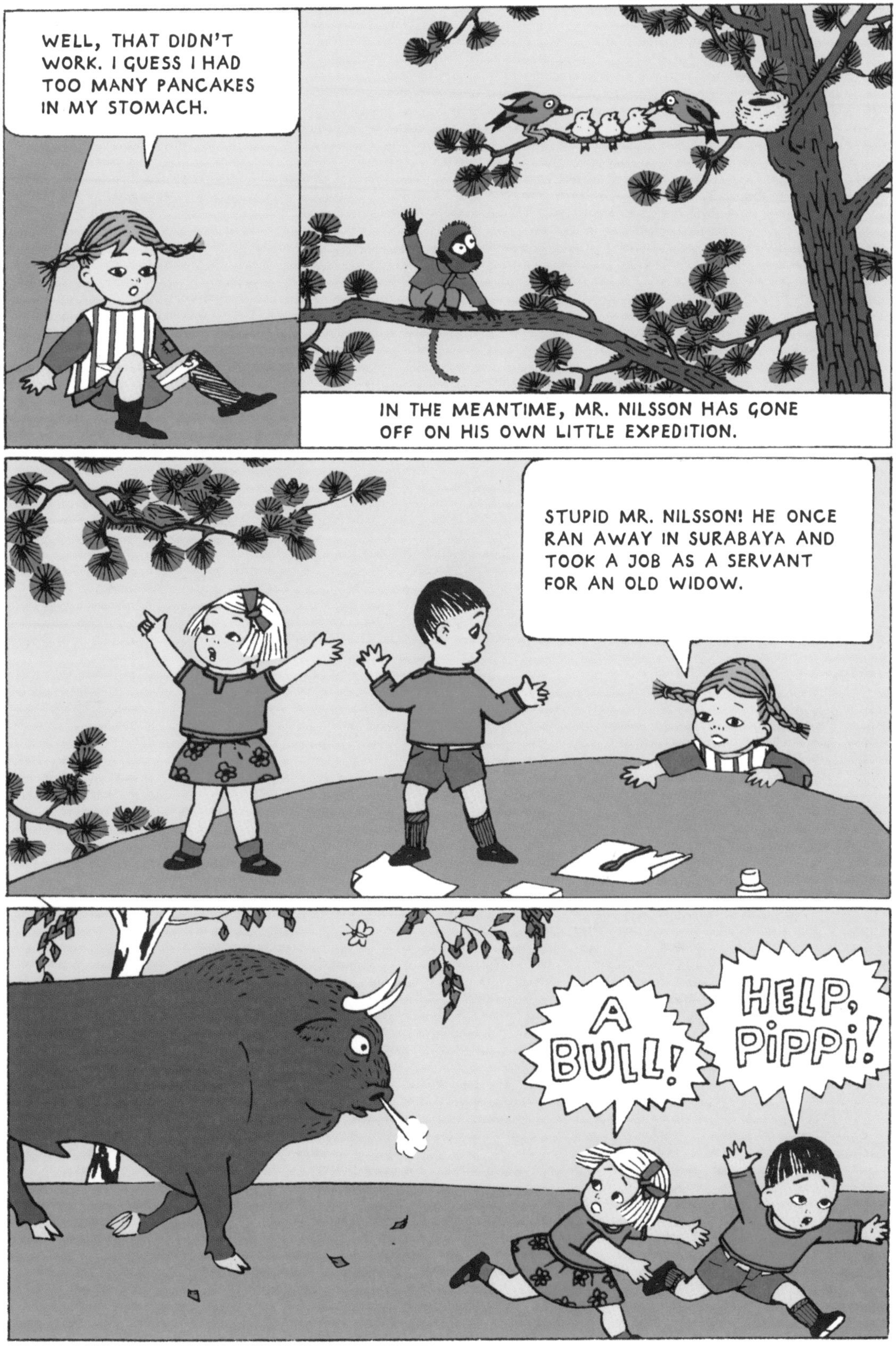
WELL, THAT DIDN'T WORK. I GUESS I HAD TOO MANY PANCAKES IN MY STOMACH.
IN THE MEANTIME, MR. NILSSON HAS GONE OFF ON HIS OWN LITTLE EXPEDITION.
STUPID MR. NILSSON! HE ONCE RAN AWAY IN SURABAYA AND TOOK A JOB AS A SERVANT FOR AN OLD WIDOW.
A BULL!
HELP, PIPPI!

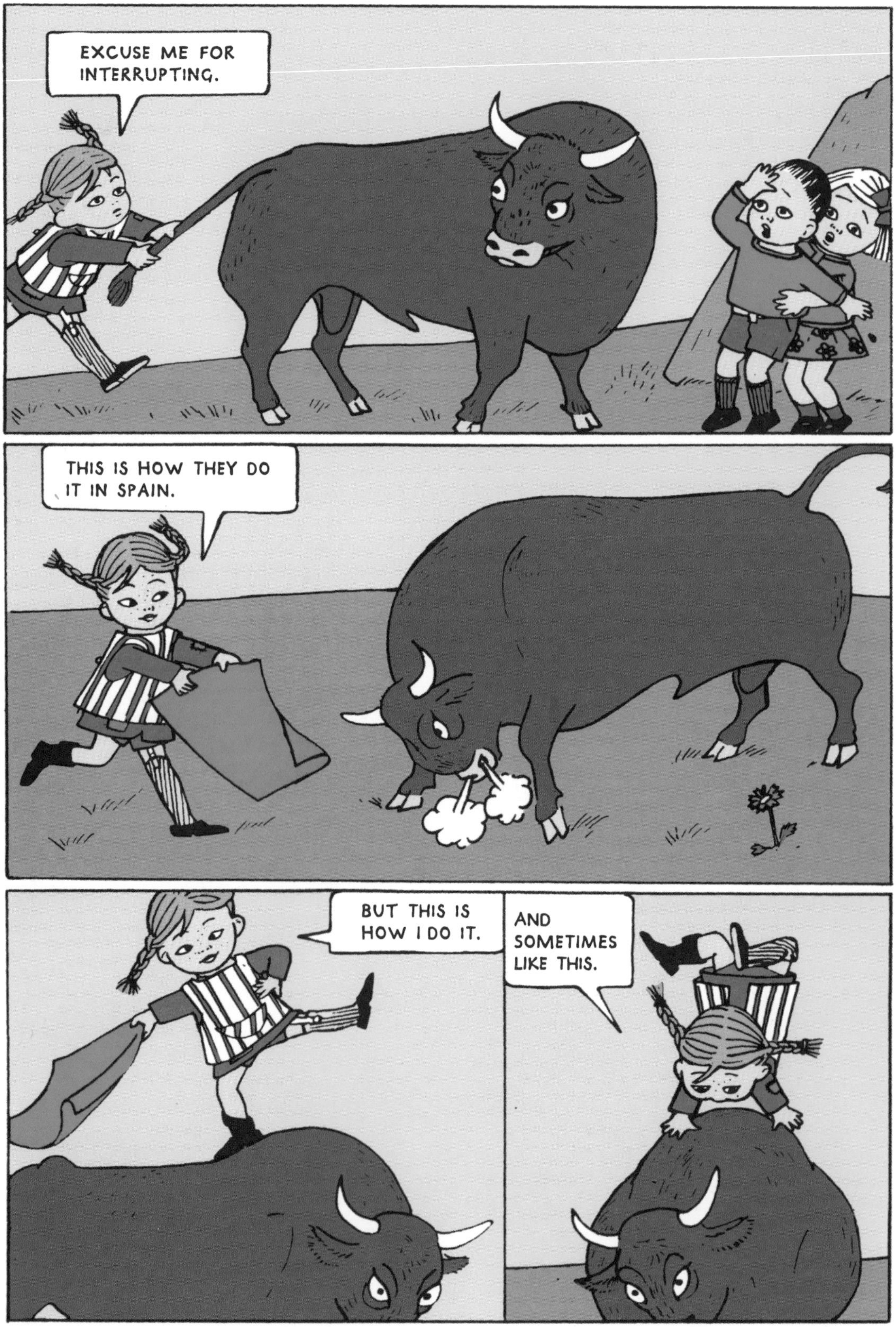
EXCUSE ME FOR INTERRUPTING.
THIS IS HOW THEY DO IT IN SPAIN.
BUT THIS IS HOW I DO IT.
AND SOMETIMES LIKE THIS.

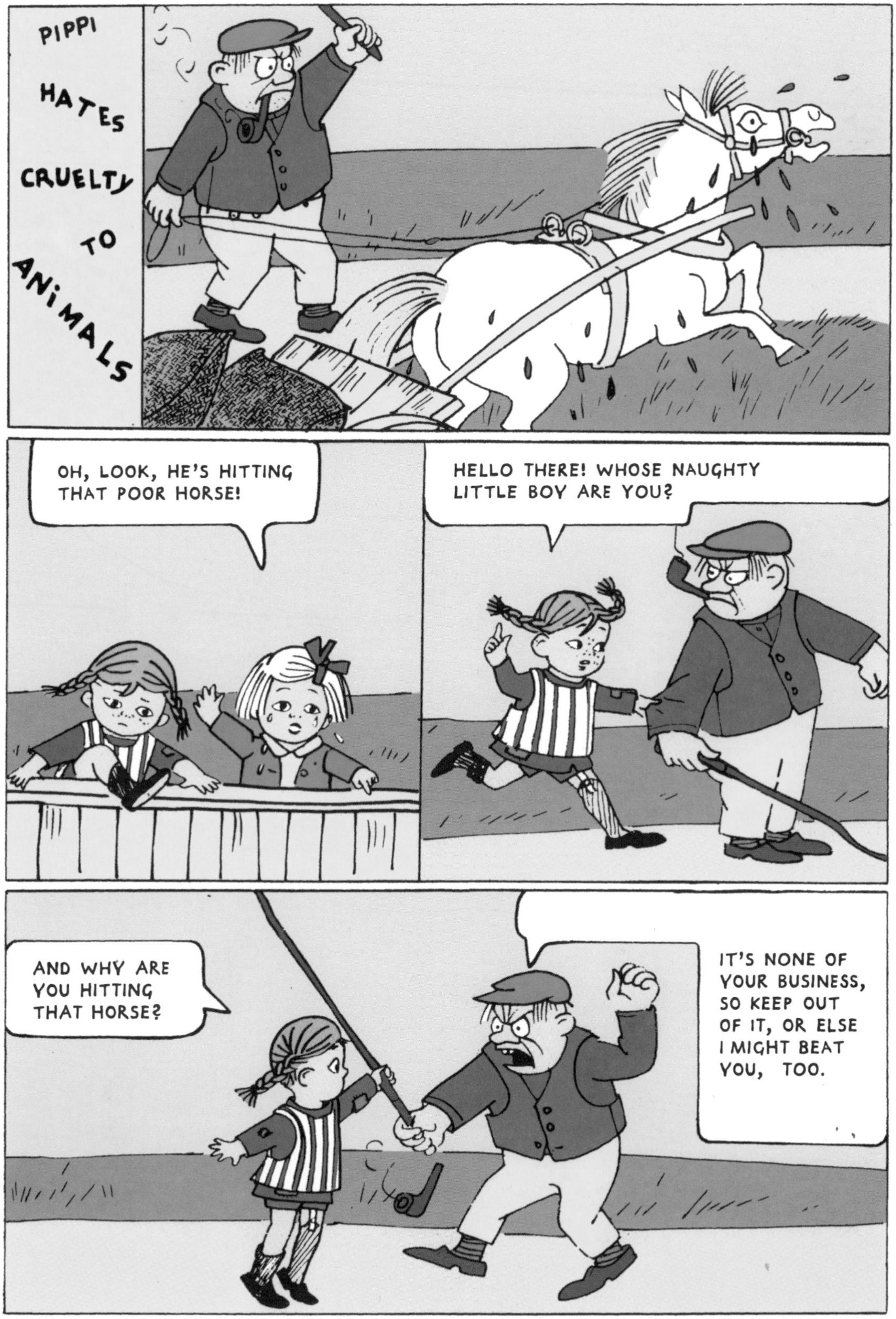
PIPPI HATES CRUELTY TO ANIMALS
OH, LOOK, HE'S HITTING THAT POOR HORSE!
HELLO THERE! WHOSE NAUGHTY LITTLE BOY ARE YOU?
AND WHY ARE YOU HITTING THAT HORSE?
IT'S NONE OF YOUR BUSINESS, SO KEEP OUT OF IT, OR ELSE I MIGHT BEAT YOU, TOO.

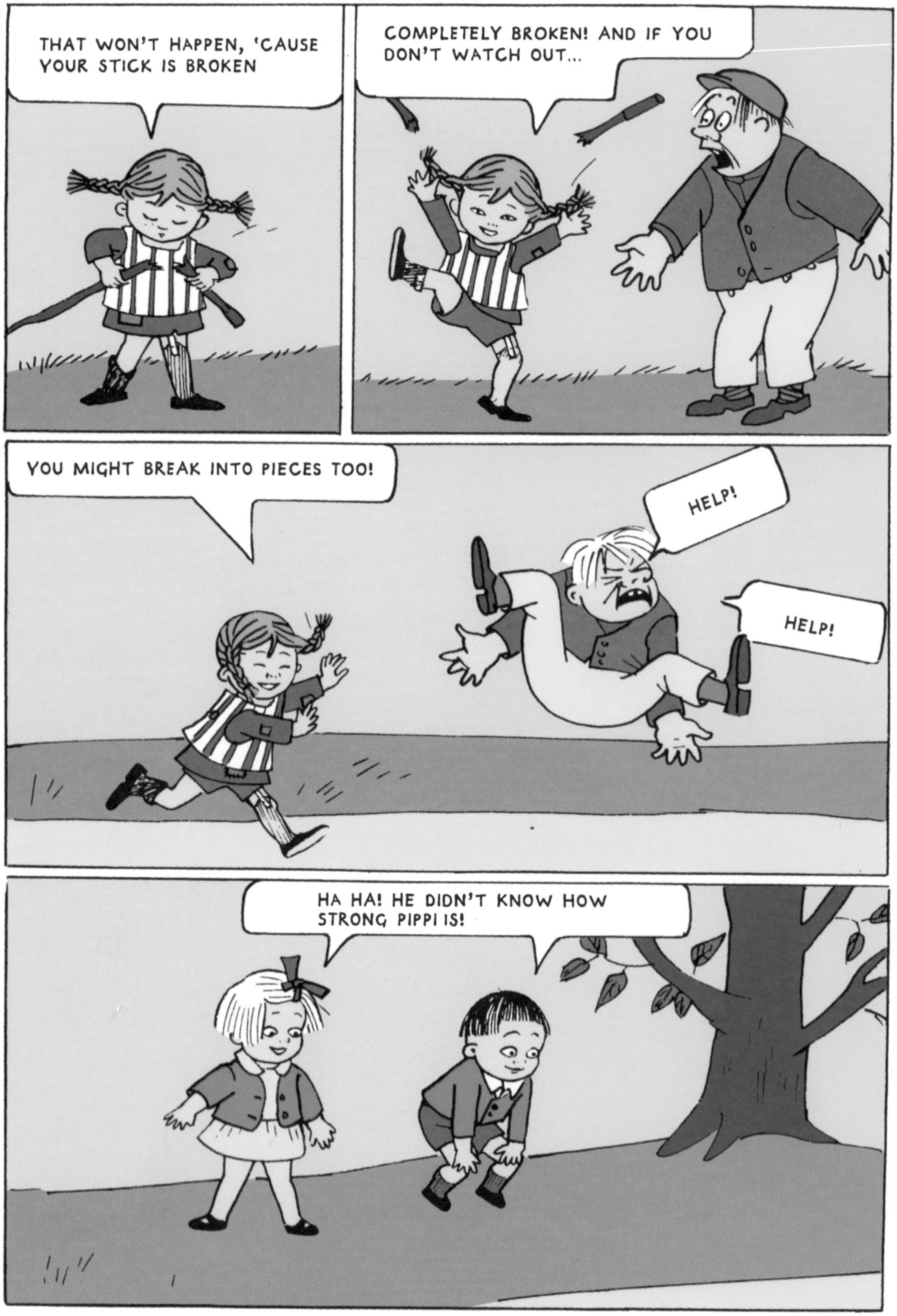

THAT WON'T HAPPEN, 'CAUSE YOUR STICK IS BROKEN
COMPLETELY BROKEN! AND IF YOU DON'T WATCH OUT...
YOU MIGHT BREAK INTO PIECES TOO!
HELP!
HELP!
HA HA! HE DIDN'T KNOW HOW STRONG PIPPI IS!

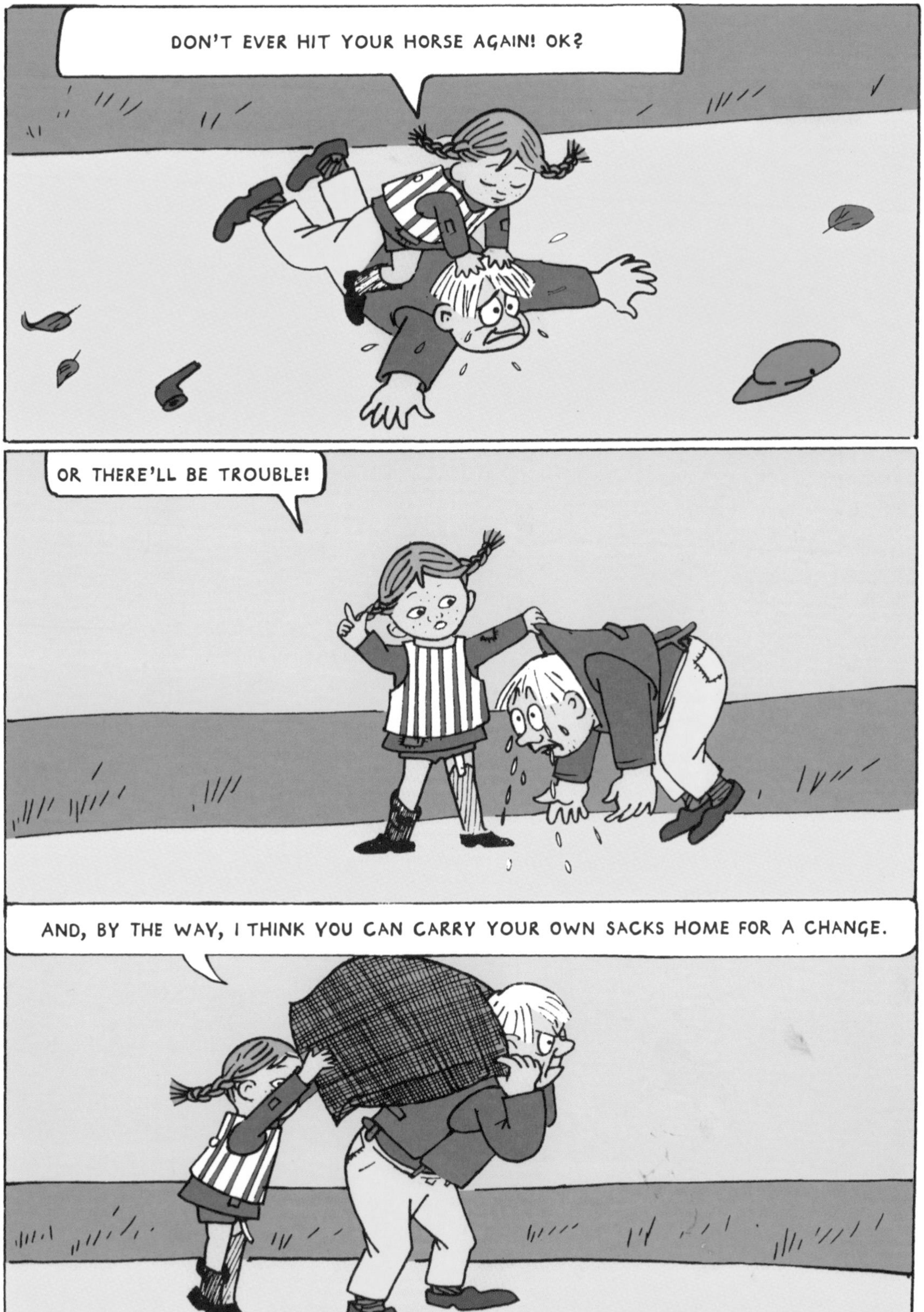
DON'T EVER HIT YOUR HORSE AGAIN! OK?
OR THERE'LL BE TROUBLE!
AND, BY THE WAY, I THINK YOU CAN CARRY YOUR OWN SACKS HOME FOR A CHANGE.

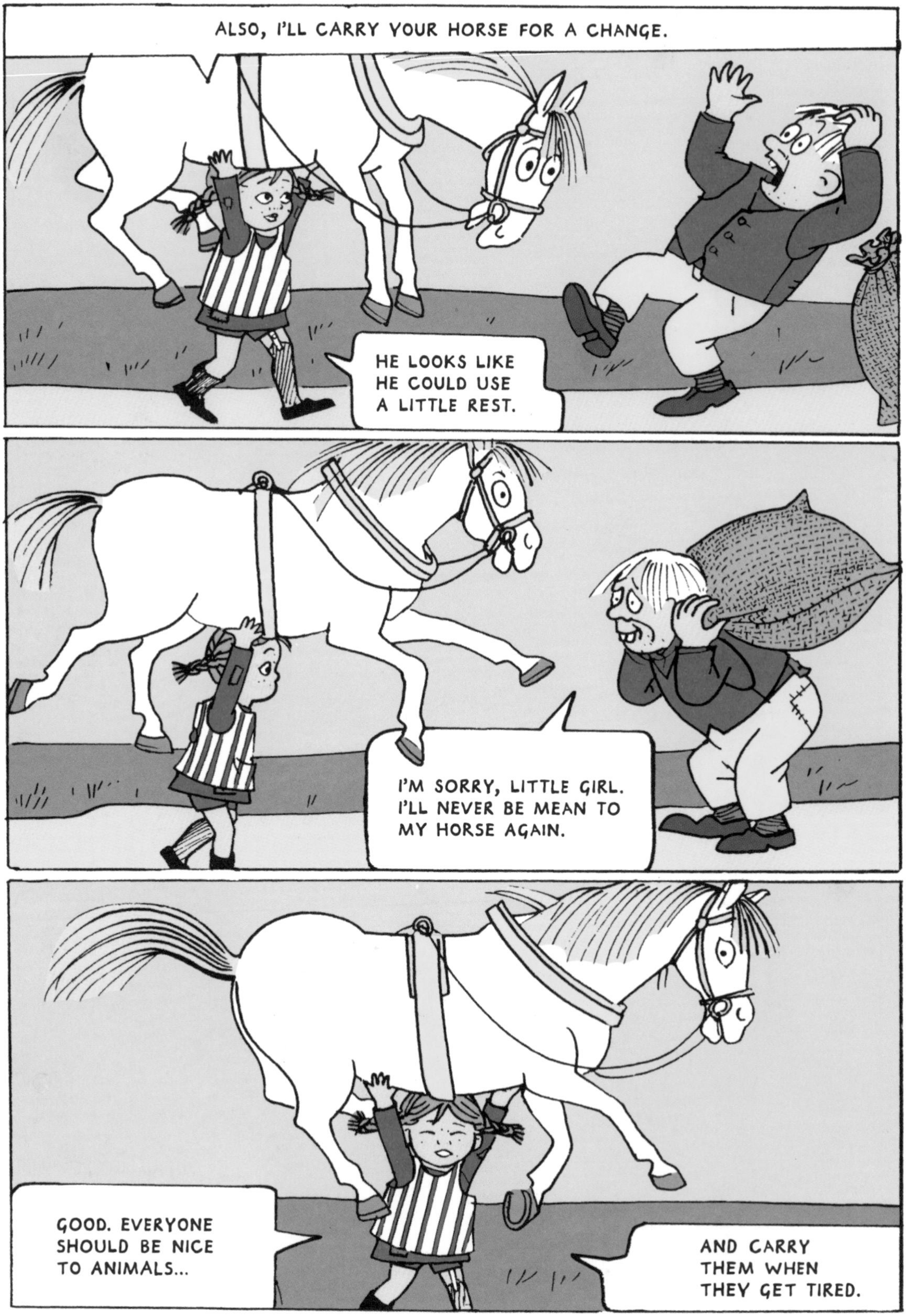
ALSO, I'LL CARRY YOUR HORSE FOR A CHANGE.
HE LOOKS LIKE HE COULD USE A LITTLE REST.
I'M SORRY, LITTLE GIRL. I'LL NEVER BE MEAN TO MY HORSE AGAIN.
GOOD. EVERYONE SHOULD BE NICE TO ANIMALS...
AND CARRY THEM WHEN THEY GET TIRED.

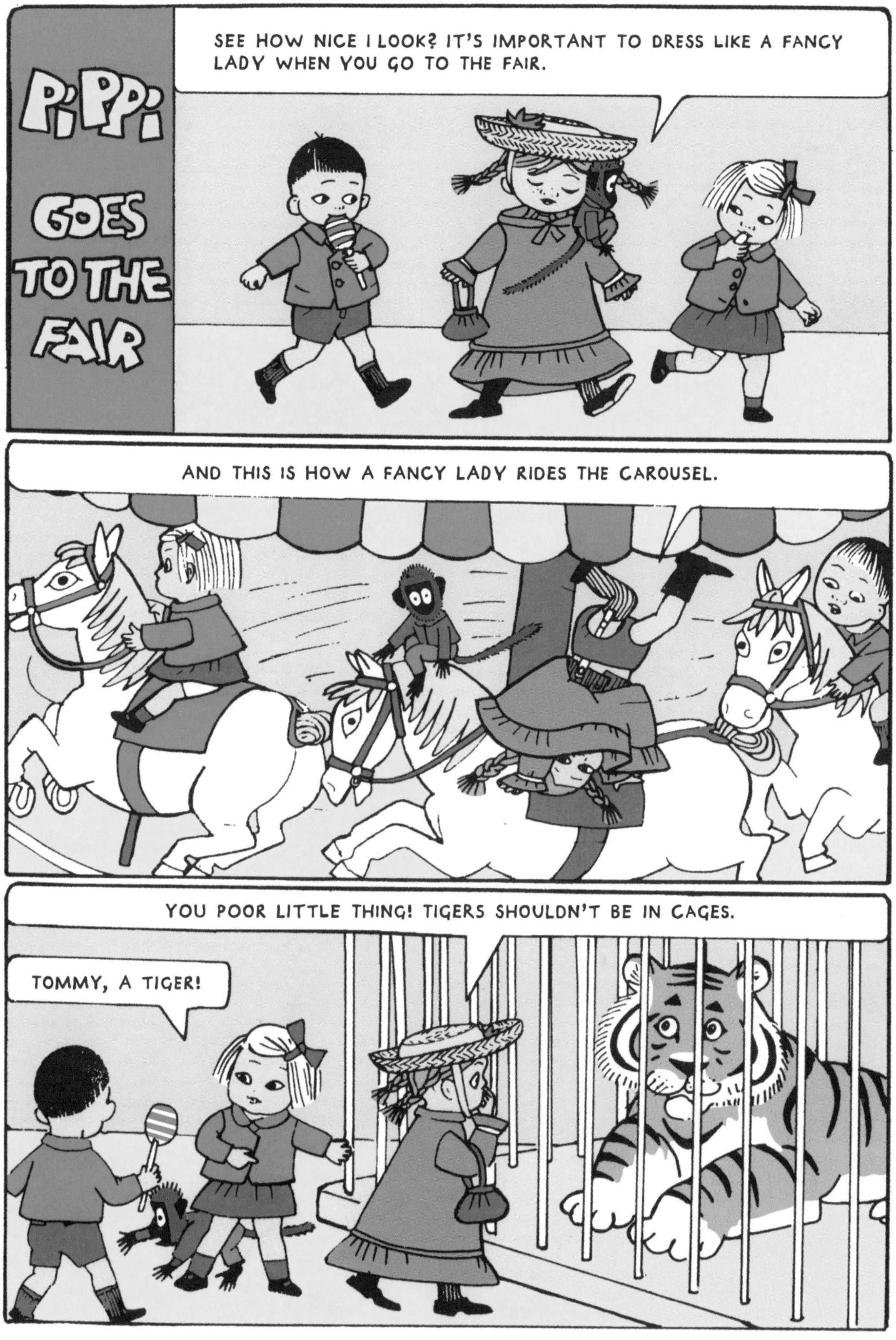
PIPPI GOES TO THE FAIR
SEE HOW NICE I LOOK? IT'S IMPORTANT TO DRESS LIKE A FANCY LADY WHEN YOU GO TO THE FAIR.
AND THIS IS HOW A FANCY LADY RIDES THE CAROUSEL.
YOU POOR LITTLE THING! TIGERS SHOULDN'T BE IN CAGES.
TOMMY, A TIGER!

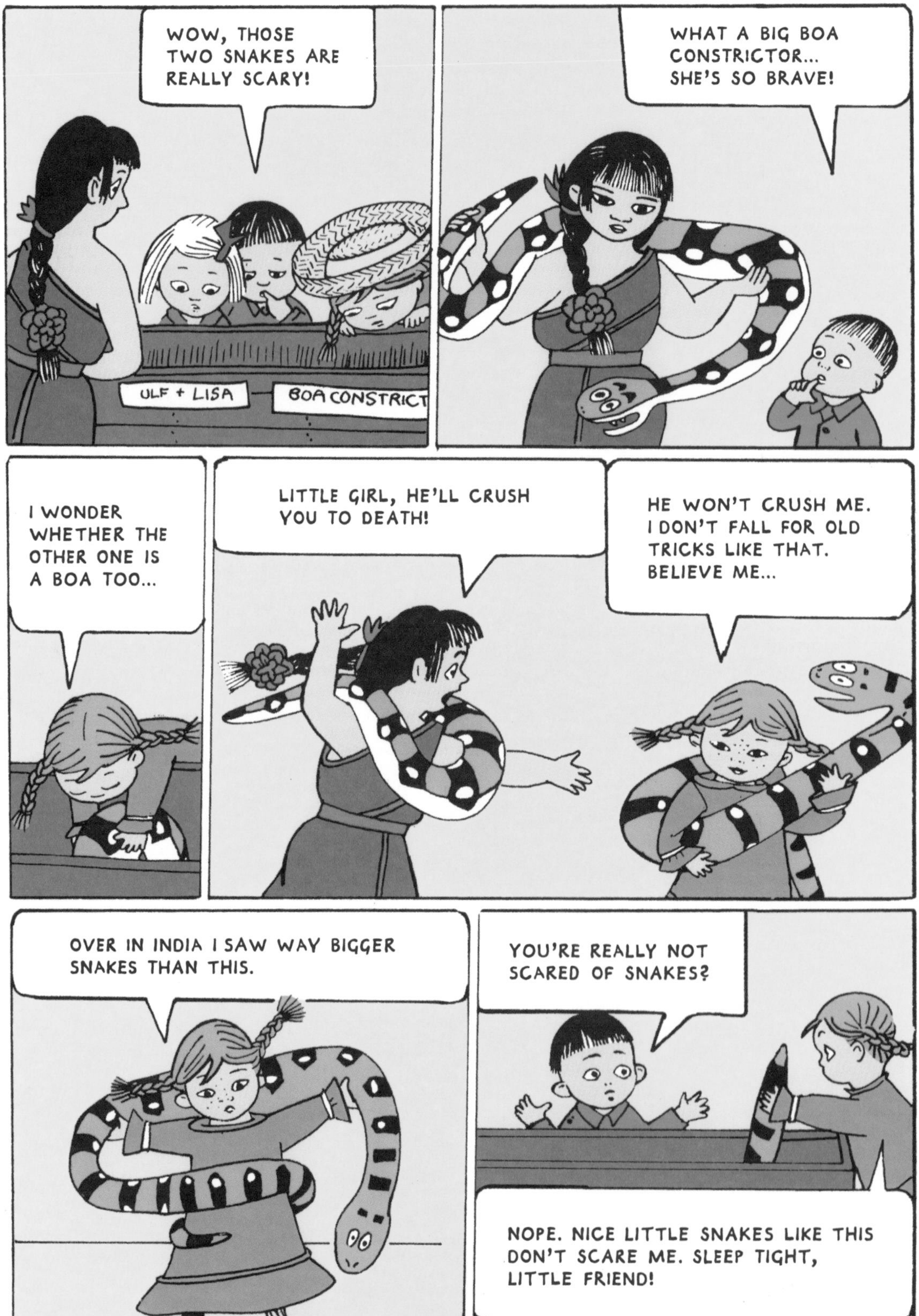
WOW, THOSE TWO SNAKES ARE REALLY SCARY!
ULF + LISA
BOA CONSTRICT
WHAT A BIG BOA CONSTRICTOR... SHE'S SO BRAVE!
I WONDER WHETHER THE OTHER ONE IS A BOA TOO...
LITTLE GIRL, HE'LL CRUSH YOU TO DEATH!
HE WON'T CRUSH ME. I DON'T FALL FOR OLD TRICKS LIKE THAT. BELIEVE ME...
OVER IN INDIA I SAW WAY BIGGER SNAKES THAN THIS.
YOU'RE REALLY NOT SCARED OF SNAKES?
NOPE. NICE LITTLE SNAKES LIKE THIS DON'T SCARE ME. SLEEP TIGHT, LITTLE FRIEND!

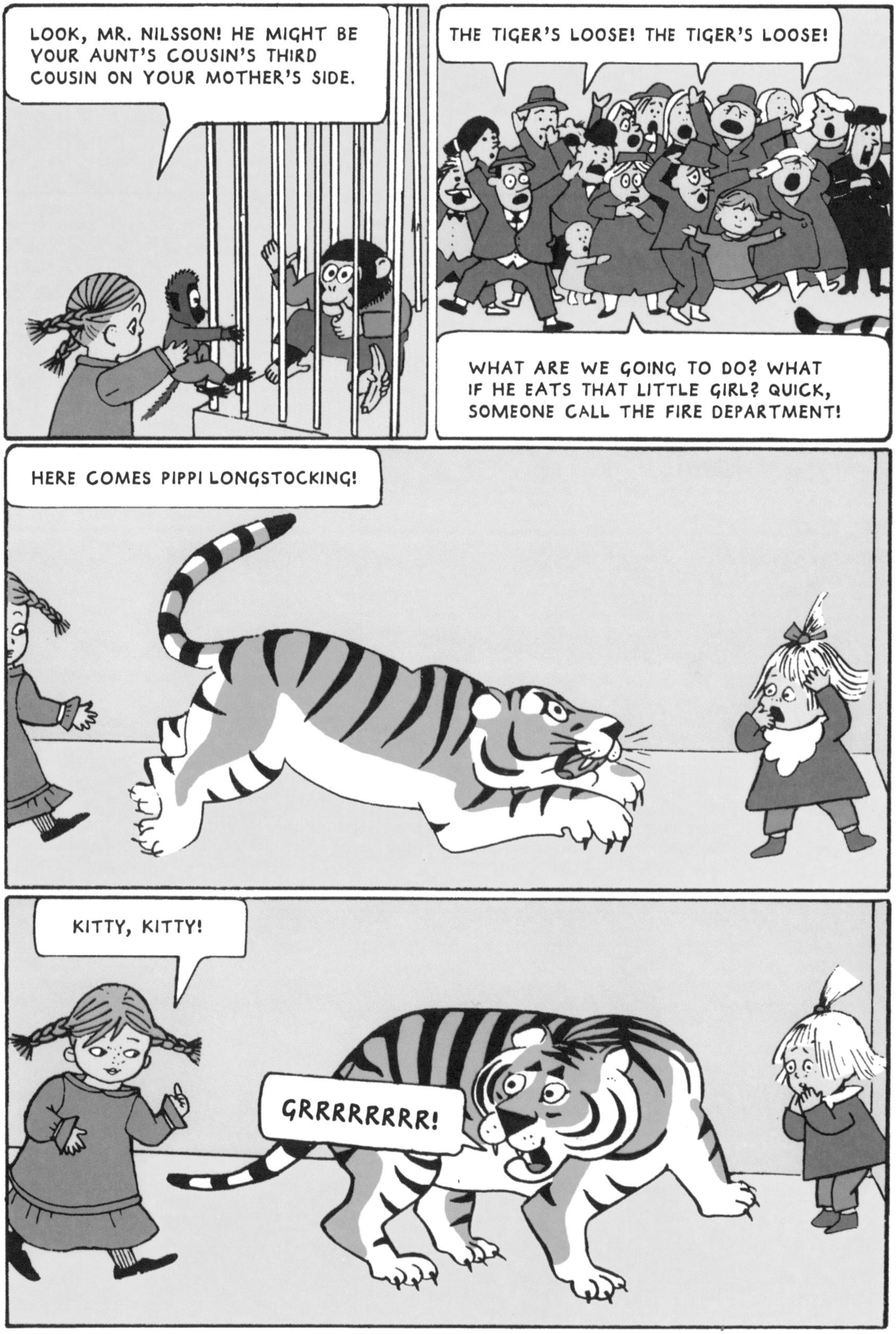
LOOK, MR. NILSSON! HE MIGHT BE YOUR AUNT'S COUSIN'S THIRD COUSIN ON YOUR MOTHER'S SIDE.
THE TIGER'S LOOSE! THE TIGER'S LOOSE!
WHAT ARE WE GOING TO DO? WHAT IF HE EATS THAT LITTLE GIRL? QUICK, SOMEONE CALL THE FIRE DEPARTMENT!
HERE COMES PIPPI LONGSTOCKING!
KITTY, KITTY!
GRRRRRRRR!

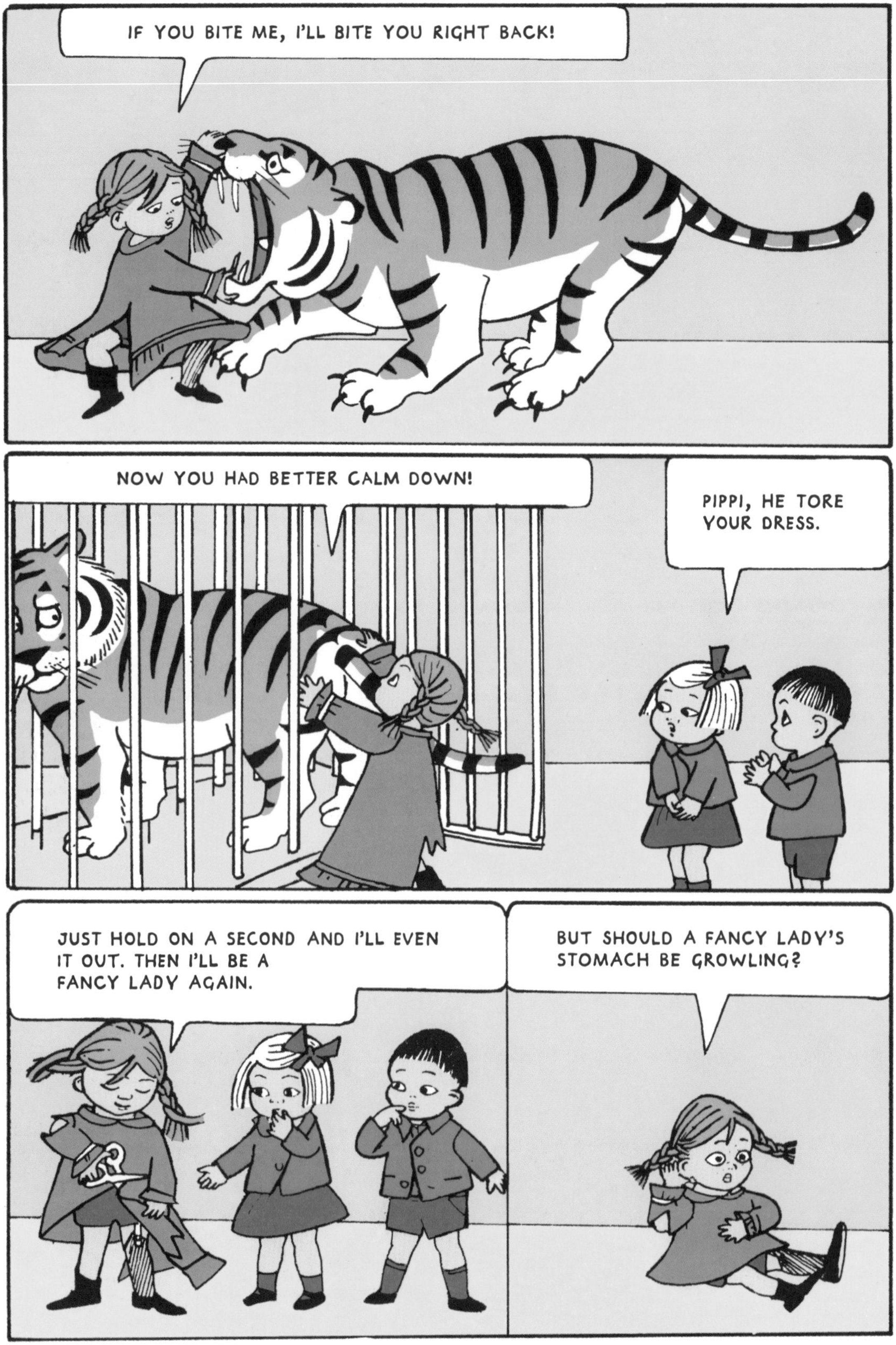
IF YOU BITE ME, I'LL BITE YOU RIGHT BACK!
NOW YOU HAD BETTER CALM DOWN!
PIPPI, HE TORE YOUR DRESS.
JUST HOLD ON A SECOND AND I'LL EVEN IT OUT. THEN I'LL BE A FANCY LADY AGAIN.
BUT SHOULD A FANCY LADY'S STOMACH BE GROWLING?

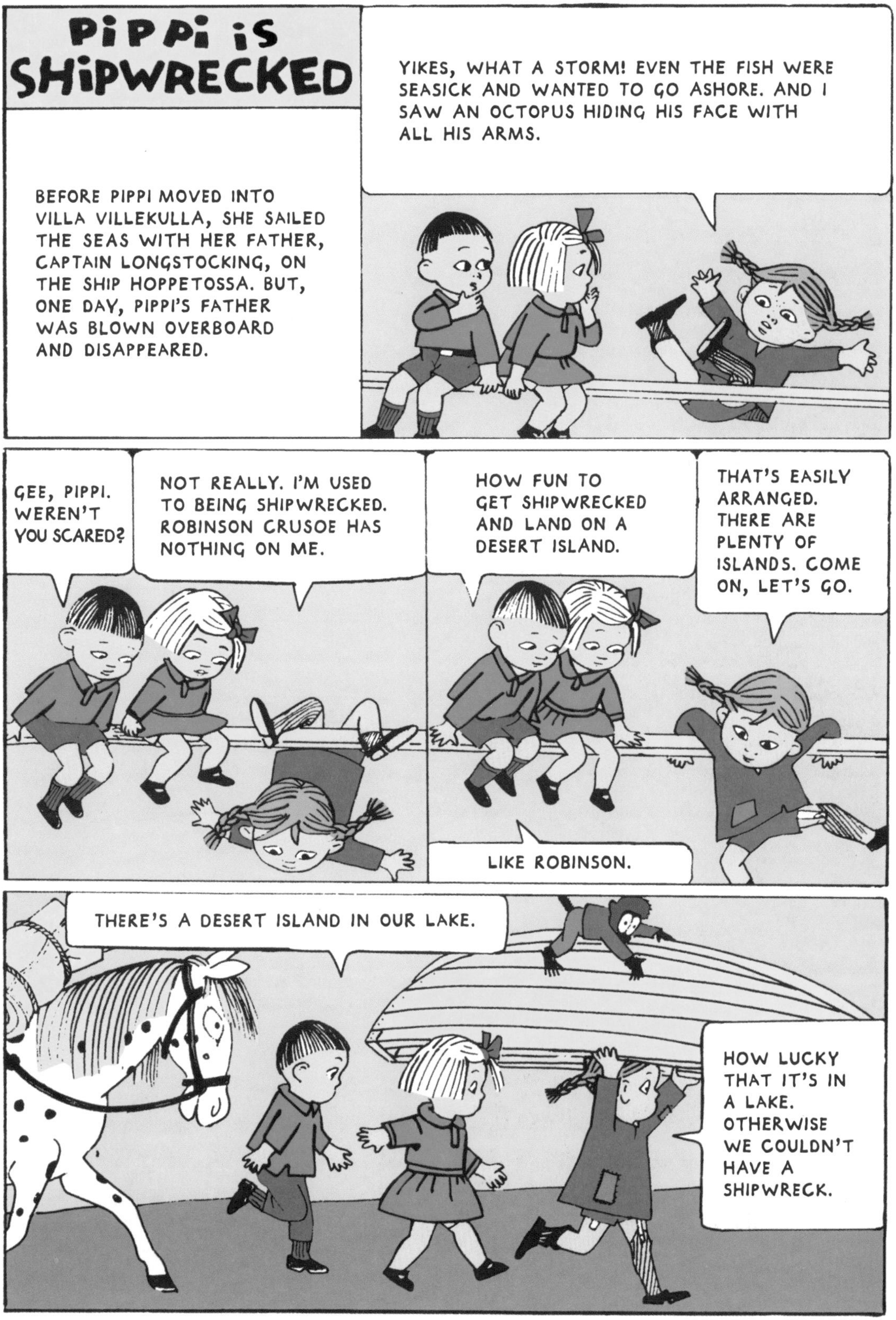
PIPPI IS SHIPWRECKED
BEFORE PIPPI MOVED INTO VILLA VILLEKULLA, SHE SAILED THE SEAS WITH HER FATHER, CAPTAIN LONGSTOCKING, ON THE SHIP HOPPETOSSA. BUT, ONE DAY, PIPPI'S FATHER WAS BLOWN OVERBOARD AND DISAPPEARED.
YIKES, WHAT A STORM! EVEN THE FISH WERE SEASICK AND WANTED TO GO ASHORE. AND I SAW AN OCTOPUS HIDING HIS FACE WITH ALL HIS ARMS.
GEE, PIPPI. WEREN'T YOU SCARED?
NOT REALLY. I'M USED TO BEING SHIPWRECKED. ROBINSON CRUSOE HAS NOTHING ON ME.
HOW FUN TO GET SHIPWRECKED AND LAND ON A DESERT ISLAND.
LIKE ROBINSON.
THAT'S EASILY ARRANGED. THERE ARE PLENTY OF ISLANDS. COME ON, LET'S GO.
THERE'S A DESERT ISLAND IN OUR LAKE.
HOW LUCKY THAT IT'S IN A LAKE. OTHERWISE WE COULDN'T HAVE A SHIPWRECK.

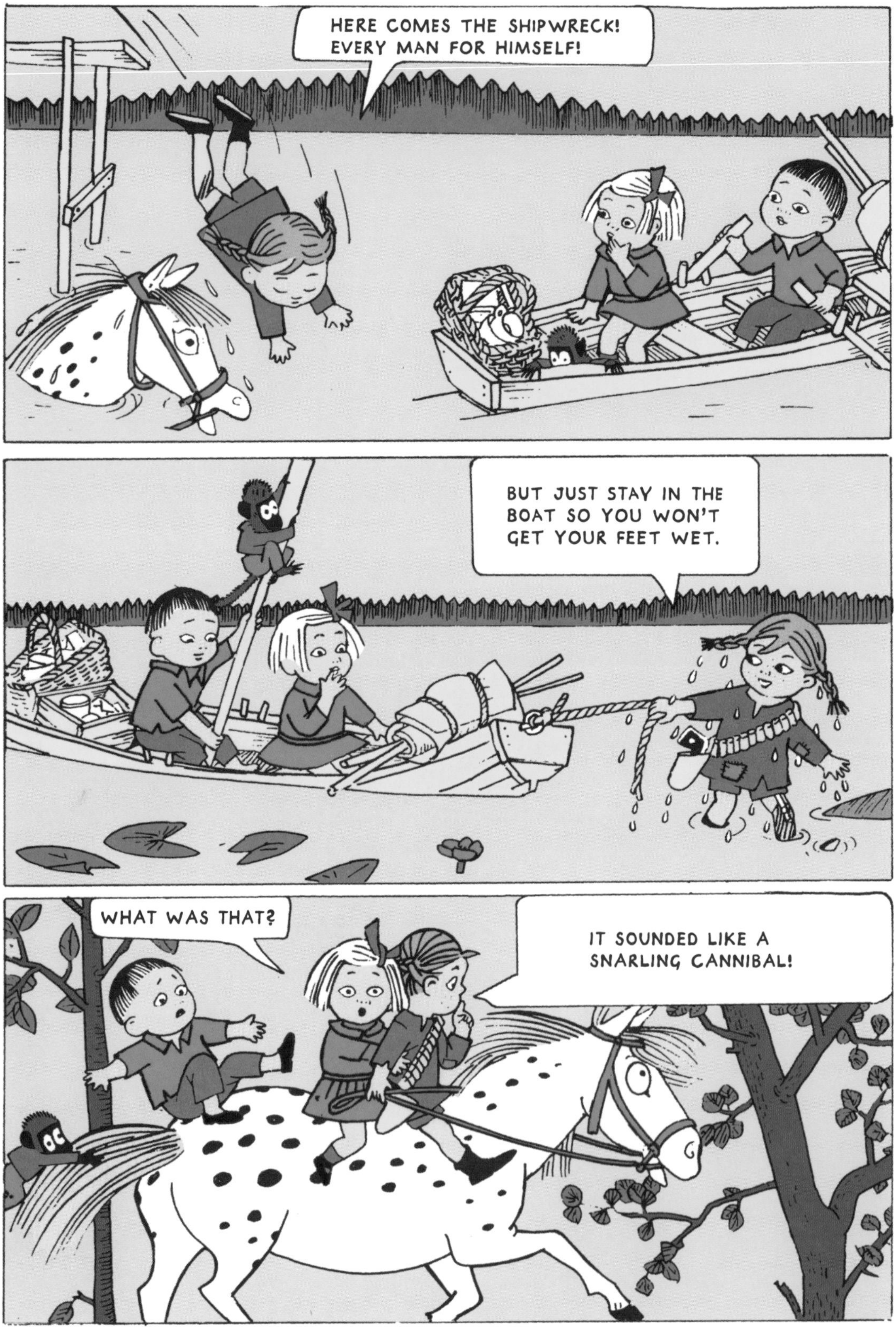
HERE COMES THE SHIPWRECK! EVERY MAN FOR HIMSELF!
BUT JUST STAY IN THE BOAT SO YOU WON'T GET YOUR FEET WET.
WHAT WAS THAT?
IT SOUNDED LIKE A SNARLING CANNIBAL!

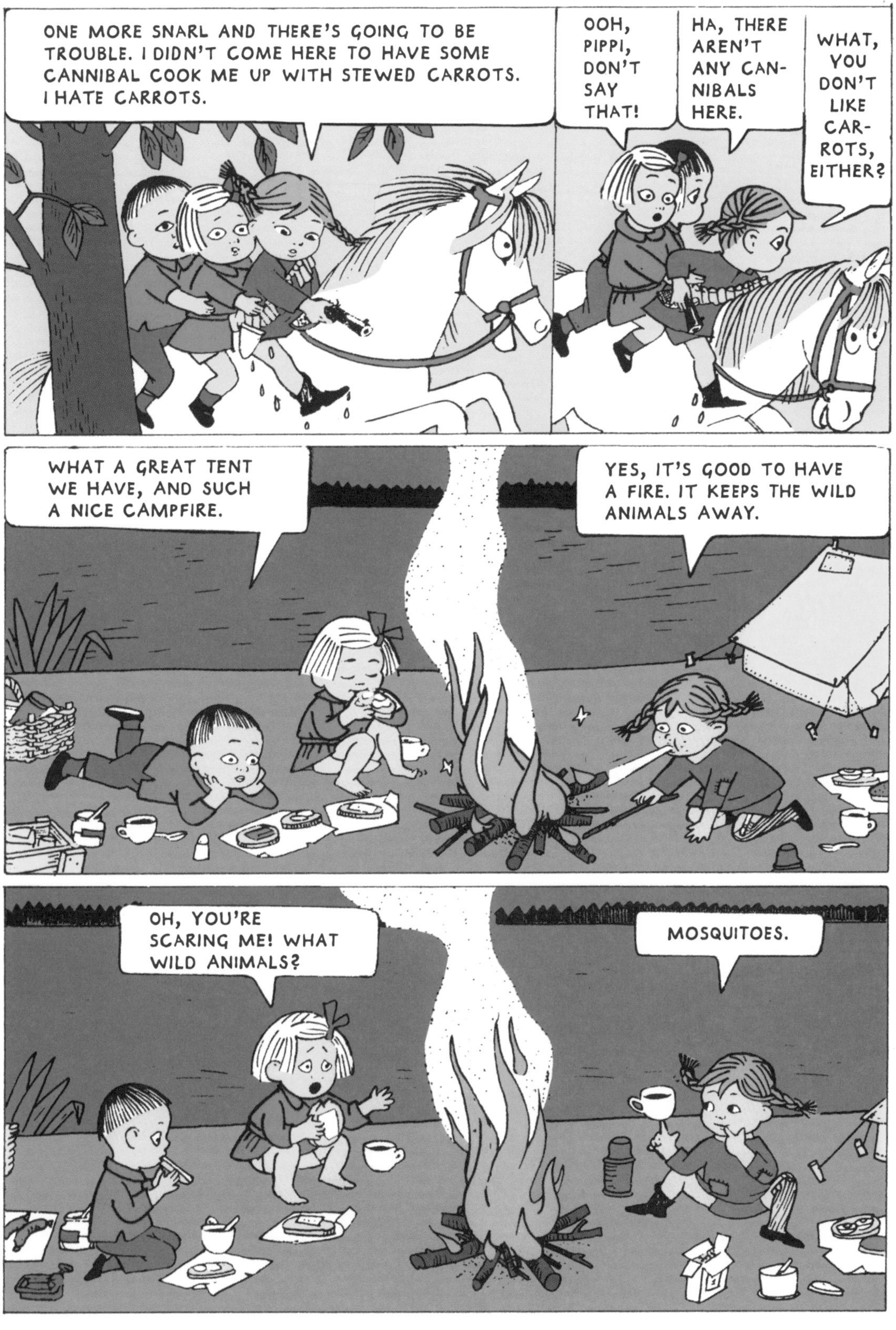
ONE MORE SNARL AND THERE'S GOING TO BE TROUBLE. I DIDN'T COME HERE TO HAVE SOME CANNIBAL COOK ME UP WITH STEWED CARROTS. I HATE CARROTS.
OOH, PIPPI, DON'T SAY THAT!
HA, THERE AREN'T ANY CAN-NIBALS HERE.
WHAT, YOU DON'T LIKE CAR-ROTS, EITHER?
WHAT A GREAT TENT WE HAVE, AND SUCH A NICE CAMPFIRE.
YES, IT'S GOOD TO HAVE A FIRE. IT KEEPS THE WILD ANIMALS AWAY.
OH, YOU'RE SCARING ME! WHAT WILD ANIMALS?
MOSQUITOES.

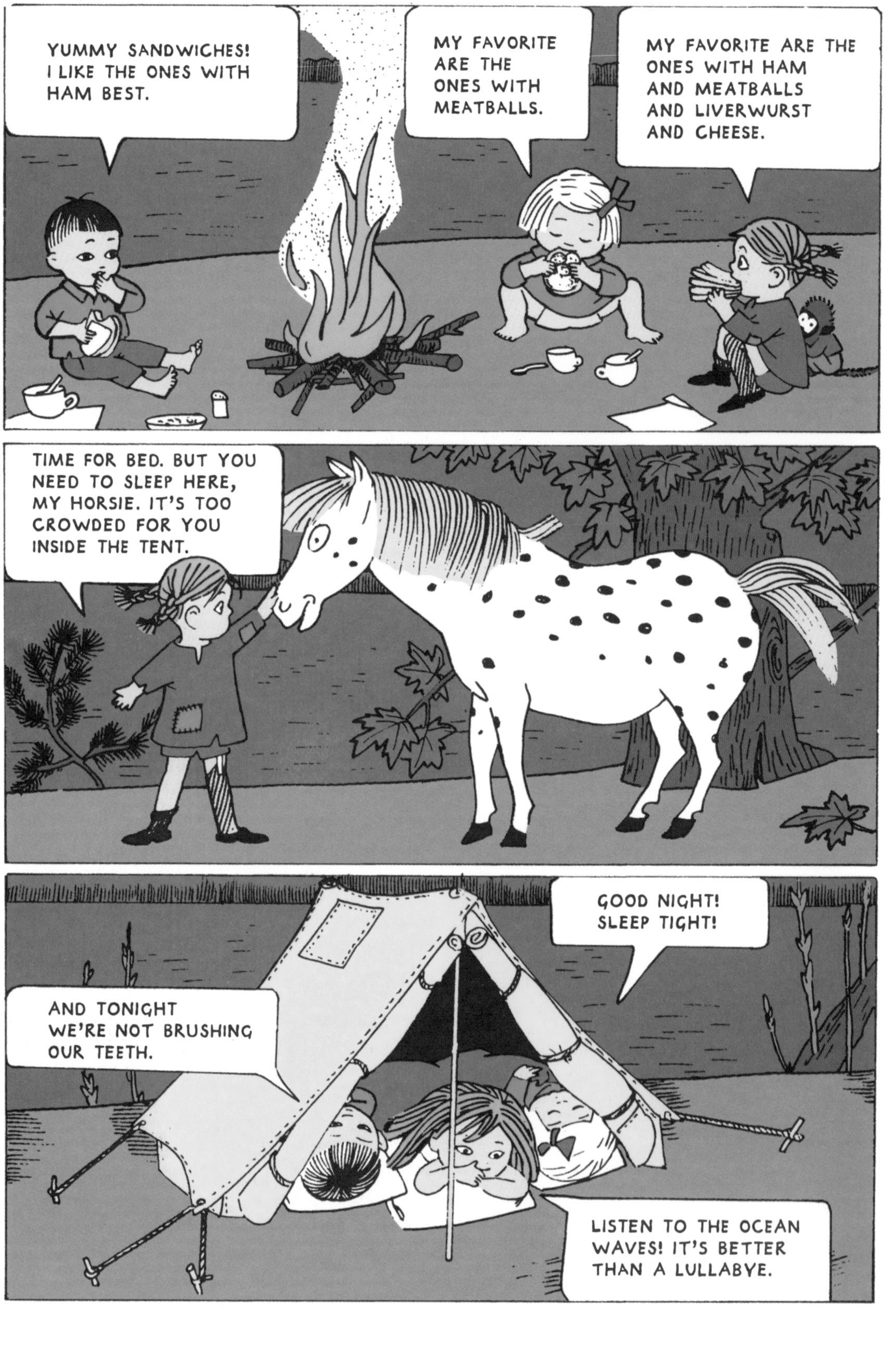
YUMMY SANDWICHES! I LIKE THE ONES WITH HAM BEST.
MY FAVORITE ARE THE ONES WITH MEATBALLS.
MY FAVORITE ARE THE ONES WITH HAM AND MEATBALLS AND LIVERWURST AND CHEESE.
TIME FOR BED. BUT YOU NEED TO SLEEP HERE, MY HORSIE. IT'S TOO CROWDED FOR YOU INSIDE THE TENT.
GOOD NIGHT! SLEEP TIGHT!
AND TONIGHT WE'RE NOT BRUSHING OUR TEETH.
LISTEN TO THE OCEAN WAVES! IT'S BETTER THAN A LULLABYE.

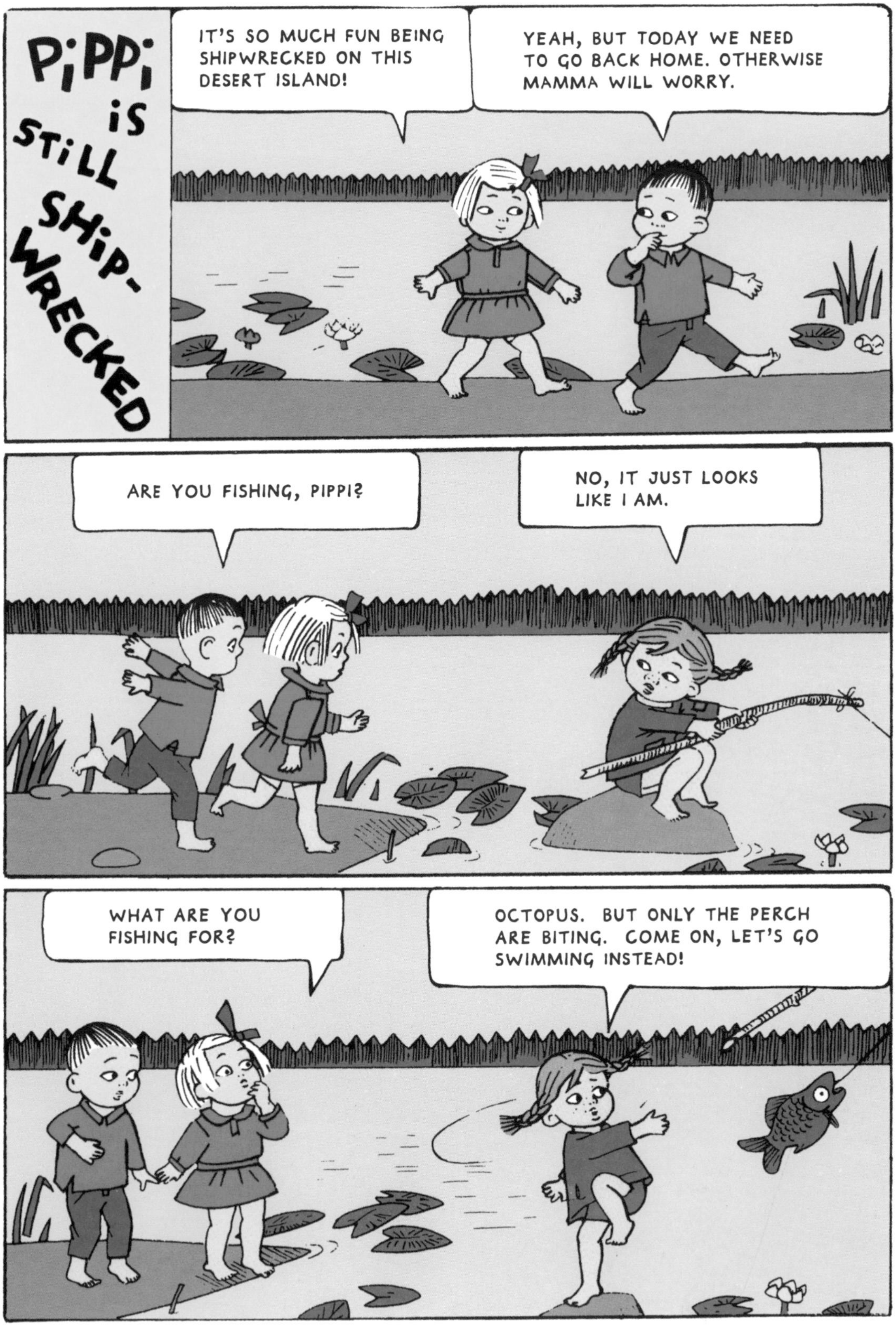
PIPPI IS STILL SHIP-WRECKED
IT'S SO MUCH FUN BEING SHIPWRECKED ON THIS DESERT ISLAND!
YEAH, BUT TODAY WE NEED TO GO BACK HOME. OTHERWISE MAMMA WILL WORRY.
ARE YOU FISHING, PIPPI?
NO, IT JUST LOOKS LIKE I AM.
WHAT ARE YOU FISHING FOR?
OCTOPUS. BUT ONLY THE PERCH ARE BITING. COME ON, LET'S GO SWIMMING INSTEAD!

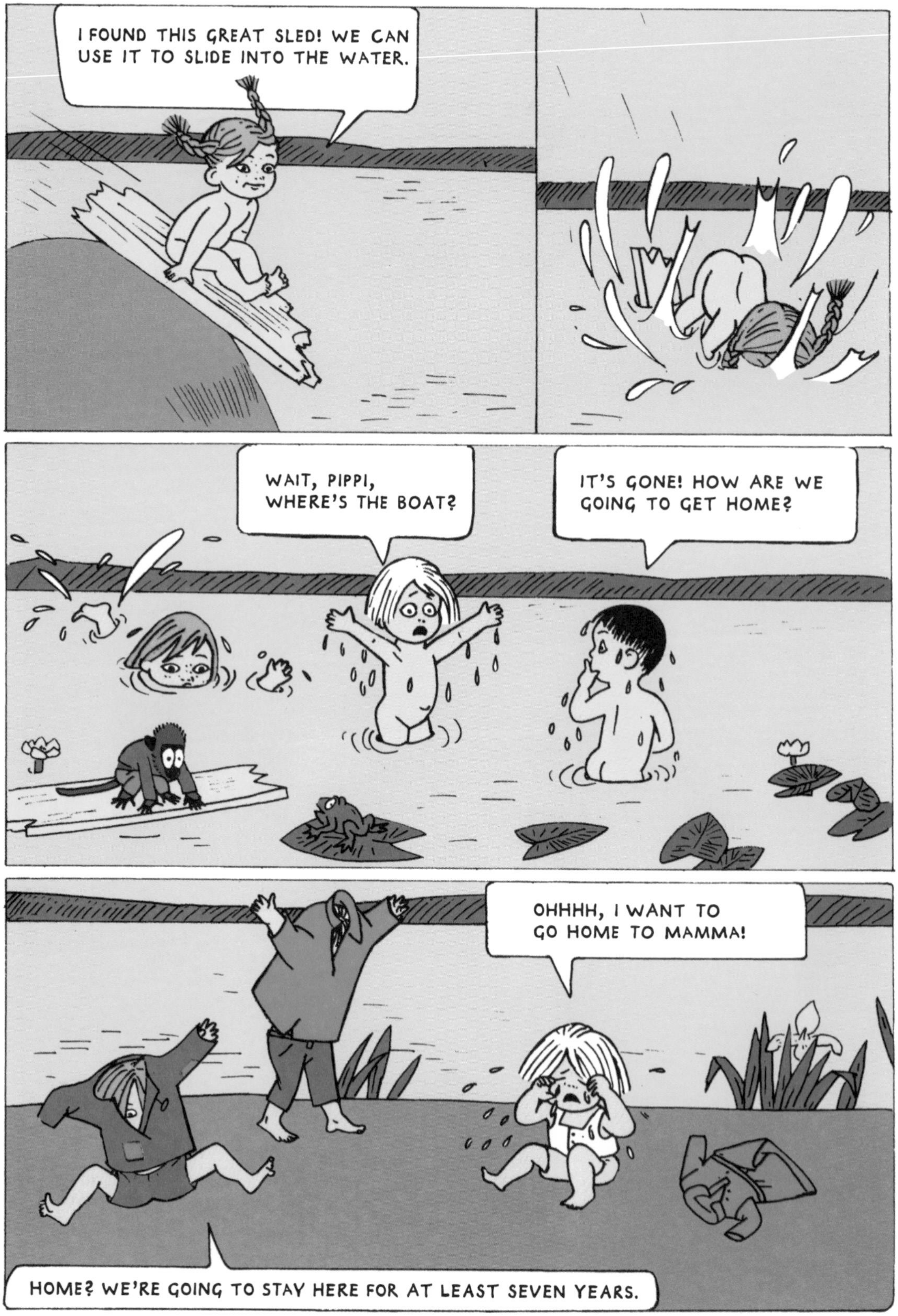
I FOUND THIS GREAT SLED! WE CAN USE IT TO SLIDE INTO THE WATER.
WAIT, PIPPI, WHERE'S THE BOAT?
IT'S GONE! HOW ARE WE GOING TO GET HOME?
OHHHH, I WANT TO GO HOME TO MAMMA!
HOME? WE'RE GOING TO STAY HERE FOR AT LEAST SEVEN YEARS.

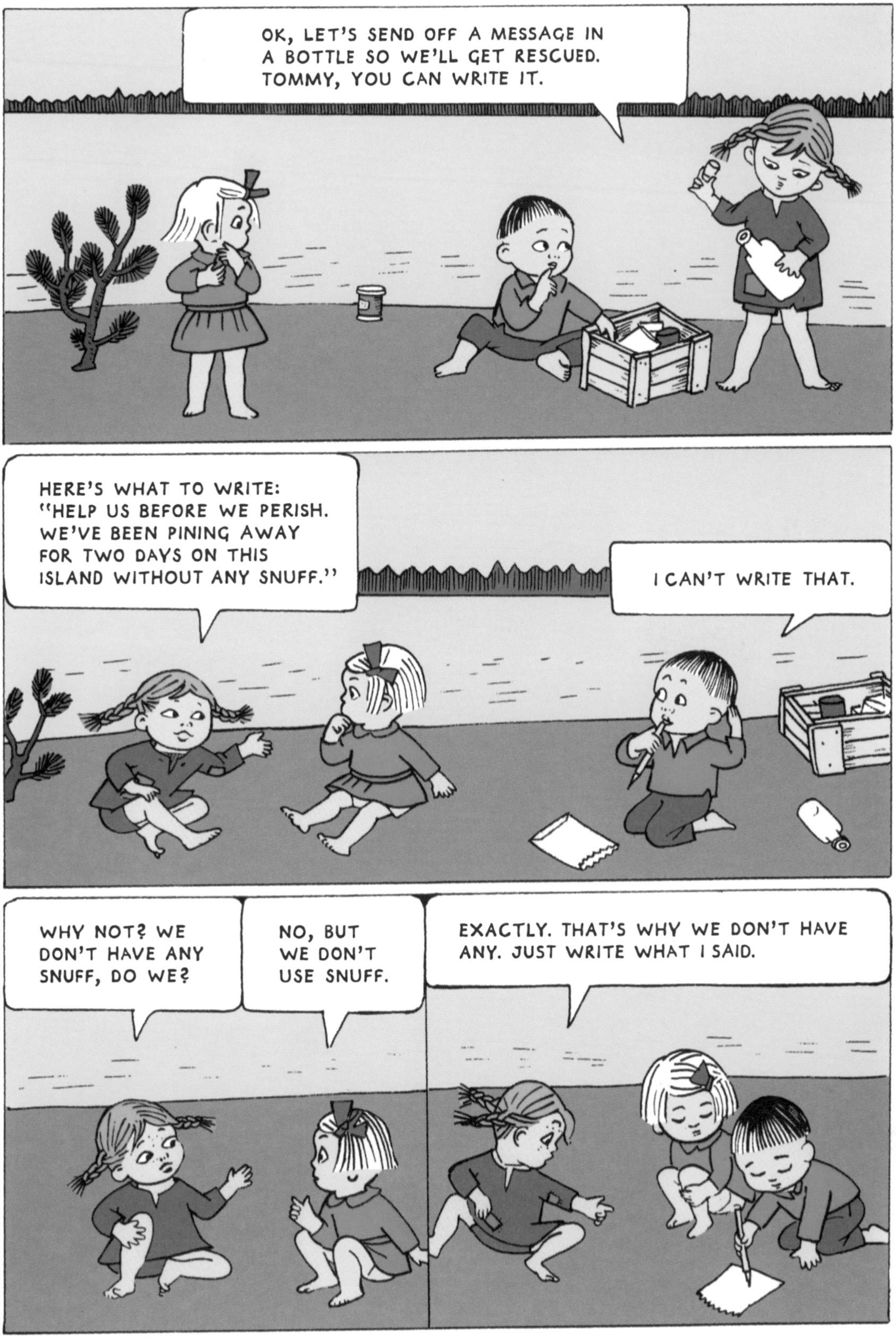
OK, LET'S SEND OFF A MESSAGE IN A BOTTLE SO WE'LL GET RESCUED. TOMMY, YOU CAN WRITE IT.
HERE'S WHAT TO WRITE: "HELP US BEFORE WE PERISH. WE'VE BEEN PINING AWAY FOR TWO DAYS ON THIS ISLAND WITHOUT ANY SNUFF."
I CAN'T WRITE THAT.
WHY NOT? WE DON'T HAVE ANY SNUFF, DO WE?
NO, BUT WE DON'T USE SNUFF.
EXACTLY. THAT'S WHY WE DON'T HAVE ANY. JUST WRITE WHAT I SAID.

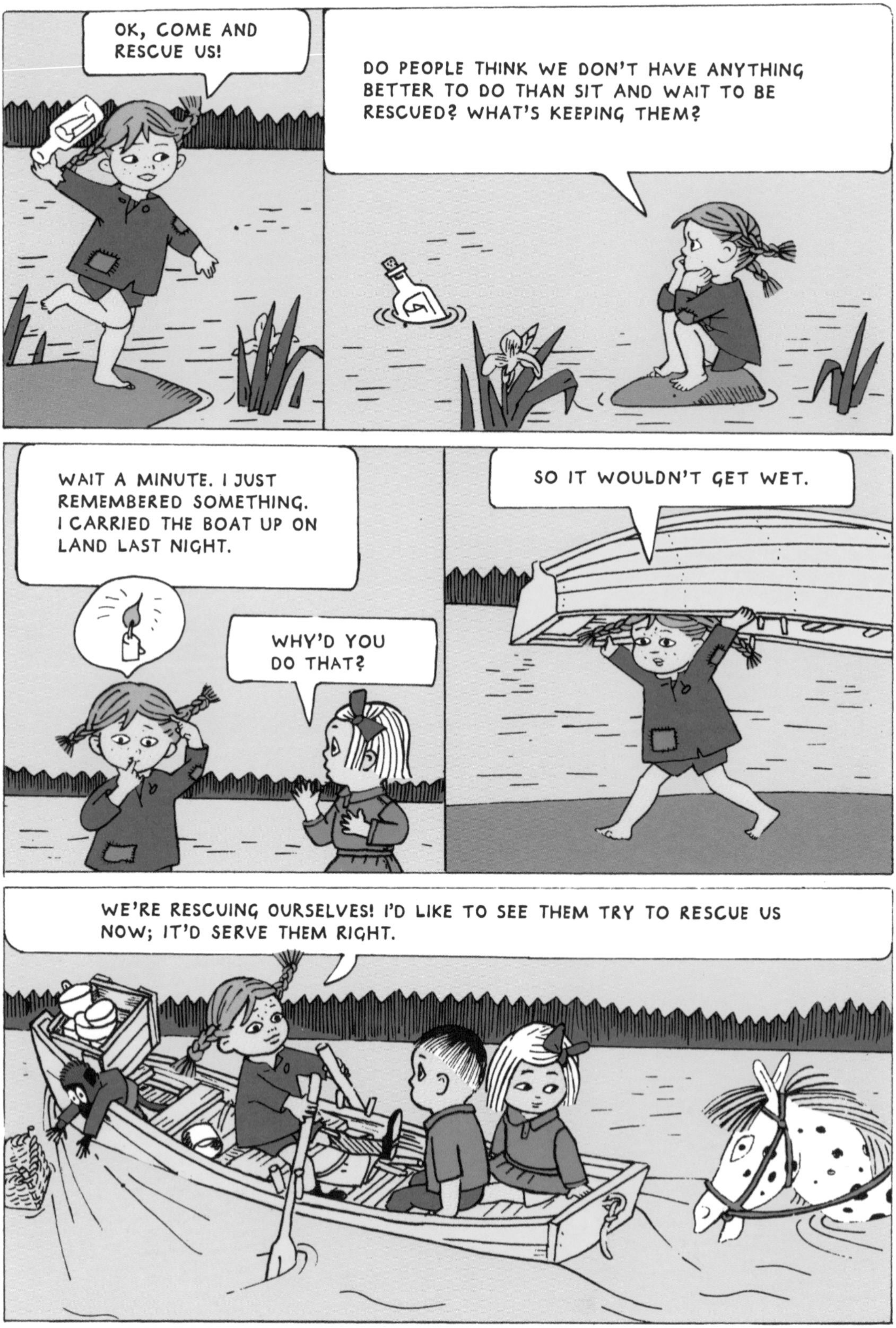
OK, COME AND RESCUE US!
DO PEOPLE THINK WE DON'T HAVE ANYTHING BETTER TO DO THAN SIT AND WAIT TO BE RESCUED? WHAT'S KEEPING THEM?
WAIT A MINUTE. I JUST REMEMBERED SOMETHING. I CARRIED THE BOAT UP ON LAND LAST NIGHT.
WHY'D YOU DO THAT?
SO IT WOULDN'T GET WET.
WE'RE RESCUING OURSELVES! I'D LIKE TO SEE THEM TRY TO RESCUE US NOW; IT'D SERVE THEM RIGHT.

Astrid Lindgren (1907-2002) was an immensely popular children's book author as well as a lifelong philanthropist. Her Pippi Longstocking series— *Pippi Longstocking* (1945), *Pippi Goes On Board* (1946), *Do You Know Pippi Longstocking?* (1947), and *Pippi in the South Seas* (1948)—has been translated into more than sixty languages and published all over the world.

During the winter of 1941, Lindgren's seven-year-old daughter Karin was ill, and asked her mother to tell her a story about Pippi Longstocking. The story Astrid Lindgren told delighted Karin and all her friends. A few years later, while recovering from an injury, Lindgren finally found the time to write down the Pippi stories. Lindgren's tenth birthday present to her daughter was the completed Pippi manuscript.

Lindgren submitted a revised version of the manuscript to the annual Rabén & Sjögren writing contest, where it won first prize. The book was published in December of 1945, and was an instant success. Rabén & Sjögren hired Lindgren as a children's book editor in 1946, and she was soon put in charge of their children's book imprint, where she worked for many years. Astrid Lindgren wrote more than seventy novels and storybooks, and has become one of the world's best loved writers with over 145 million books sold worldwide.

Ingrid Vang Nyman (1916-1959) was a Danish-born illustrator who was best known for her work on Swedish children's books. As a child, she suffered from tuberculosis, and at age thirteen, she lost vision in one eye.

Vang Nyman studied at the Royal Danish Academy of Fine Arts in Copenhagen before she moved to Stockholm, where her career in children's book illustration took off. She was briefly married to the poet and painter Arne Nyman, with whom she had a son named Peder. When the marriage ended in 1944, Ingrid Vang Nyman began a relationship with the lawyer and author Uno Eng. It was also around this time that she created the first images of Pippi Longstocking. The feisty Pippi was no doubt somewhat of a kindred spirit with Vang Nyman, who had a strong faith in her own abilities, something not especially common among children's book illustrators of the day. Ingrid Vang Nyman went on to illustrate numerous children's books over the course of her brief career.

Tiina Nunnally is widely considered to be the preeminent translator from Scandinavian languages into English. Her many awards and honors include the PEN/ BOMC Translation Prize for her work on Sigrid Undset's *Kristin Lavransdatter*. She grew up in Milwaukee and received an M.A. in Scandinavian Studies from the University of Wisconsin.

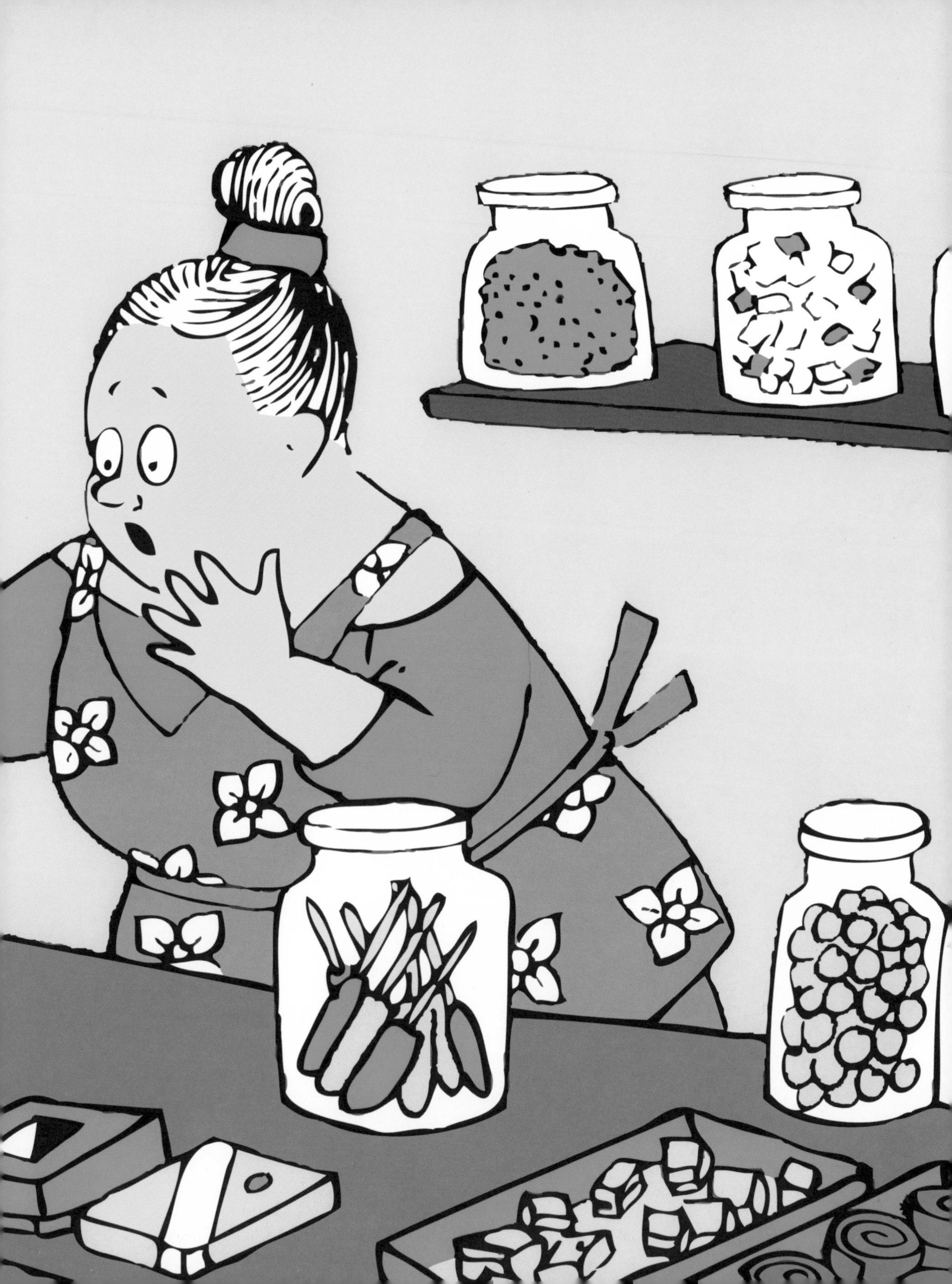

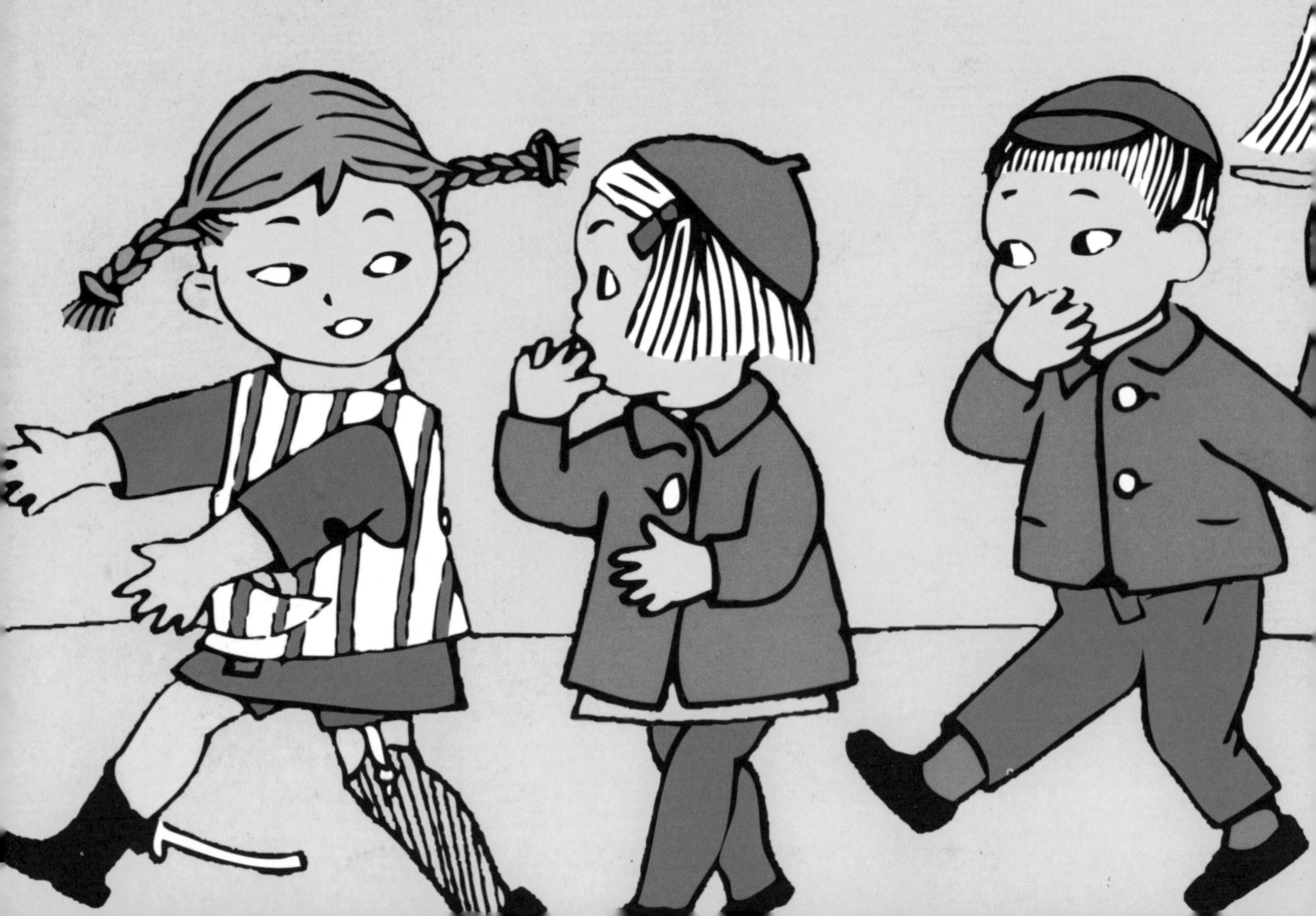